LE   TO

RACHEL

R. W. Mitchell

To my dear mum, for writing to me every week for the past 3 years and for being my true inspiration in life.

CONTENTS

ACKNOWLEDGMENTS

I would like to thank the following people for supporting me and providing me with the inspiration in life to write 'Letters to Rachel'.

My wonderful family
Alexa Seaman
Alison Bensalhia
Barbra Clarke
Daniel Farrugia
David Martin
Emma Reeves-Luker
Erhan Kalyon
Gwendal Hamon
Jacqui Capuano
Jo Edwards
Julie Connelly
Kate Hillier
Keri Davies
Laura Steer
Lucy Pastor Hayden
Madeline Palmer
Manuel Román
Nico Stévenoot
Phil Shaw
Raschid Aoudia
Sarah Rose
Serena Jones
Victor Hernadez
Everyone at GAPS
Everyone at Storrington Dramatic Society

With special thanks to Graham Howe and Elaine Stadnicki for bringing 'Letters to Rachel' alive!

Chapter 1
August - Hola / Good bye

1st August

Dear Rachel,

Well, my dear darling, I can't believe you've done it! You've flown the nest and not to a nearby nest but all the way to Spain! Bet you're already sunning yourself on the terrace with a glass of sangria in your hand. (I know I certainly would be, if your Father would let me!)

Your leaving party was rather fun, wasn't it? The music wasn't really our cup of tea... not even sure what a 'Hangman Style' really is, sweetie, but your father seemed to enjoy himself. You do have a lovely group of friends and I'm sure they'll all be out to visit you in next to no time. Perhaps don't give your address to that awful Victoria Plum woman, though. I swear she's the most boring woman I've ever met - and don't get me started on her drippy husband! Terrible outfit too; did she think it was fancy dress?! I've seen better-dressed characters in EastEnders. Anyway apart from her, we had a great 'mingle'. That Marcus is a lovely man isn't he? Quite dashing too. He obviously is very fond of you darling, couldn't keep his eyes off you. Shame nothing worked out while you were here. Anyway 'plenty more fish' and all that, and I'm sure Barcelona will be filled with plenty of 'hotties', as your friends call them.

Sorry I didn't come to the airport but I just couldn't face it. I was happy being a soppy old mess here at home but being like that at the airport just wouldn't do at all. Your father said you got off all right, which is the main thing. Said there was one of those

1

terrible 'Stag Do's' on your flight. Hope you weren't anywhere near them. Personally I find them terribly common. When your father and I got married he had a much more civilized 'do' down the 'Dog and Partridge' with Uncle Jim and Bertie. Poor old Bertie, still haven't got over him. Best dog we've ever had.

Once you've settled into your 'el flato', please give me a buzz, darling, or else you know I'll worry. The odd photo of you on the beach in your bathing suit would also be lovely. I always have a space on my fridge for my best girl.

Anyway must head off. Your father has just arrived home with a new lawnmower and I'll need to supervise him before he electrocutes Himself - or worse still, ruins my front lawn!

Love, peace and happiness,

Mum and Dad xxx

P.S: The party food was amazing, you really are a talented baker, the cakes especially were delicious! Where did those vols-au-vent come from though? They were so tasty that your father and I did a pincer movement on the poor waitress so we got a good plateful each!

5th August

Dear Mum and Dad,

Thanks for the letter I loved it. It was my first letter to my 'el flato'. So nice to open the post and find a letter instead of a stack of bills. Mind you, I'm not sure you needed five first class stamps on the envelope. I'm only in Spain, not China!

Well, after our brief phone call I did indeed sit on the terrace and had a large mojito; you'd like one of those, mum, they're a bit like a minty version of Dad's summer punch's (only less alcoholic!).

Glad you enjoyed the leaving party. Fab wasn't it? I wasn't too red and puffy from crying all night, was I? Suz said I looked like I had been watching "Love Actually" the night after Peter broke up with me! Cow! Lol! .....and I don't know what you mean about Marcus Flynn; he hardly talked to me all night. Think he must have been distracted by Victoria Plum's awful dress! And yes, Mum, she will be sent the wrong address so I never have to see her again. Ever! How I worked with that woman for 6 years without throwing something at her I'll never know!

3

Don't worry about not coming to the airport, mum; as I said on the phone, we had our special goodbye together and that was perfect. I'm wearing the necklace you bought me. It's gorgeous! I do believe that if it's matched with a nice top, I'll look quite the 'chic chica' as I wander around the streets of Barcelona.

Oh yes, the flight was quite an event! It wasn't just a stag do that I was sat in between; it was a rugby team stag do! Let's just say I now know all six verses of Sweet Chariot (and it isn't the version you know!)

The 'el flato' is looking minimal, you could say. My boxes still haven't arrived! Sob! It's been 8 days now and I'm on my 3rd cycle of the one suitcase of clothes I brought with me on the plane. I swear if they don't arrive soon I'll be wearing the ghastly flat curtains in a toga style, just so that I'm not seen out in the same 4 outfits again! Perhaps you could give the company a buzz for me and put the pressure on. I always crumble when I deal with people on the phone. You have my full permission to give 'The Big Parcel Company' a right good telling off. Get my boxes to me mum! I couldn't bear it if someone in Denmark was unpacking my zebra-patterned cushion covers!

Anyway must dash. Heading down the beach for a lush dip in the sea before dinner tonight.

Love Rachel xxx

P.S: They eat terribly late here. 10pm!!! At the moment I have to eat a supper at 7pm then dinner at 10pm or else I'd be totally famished! Better get out of that habit though otherwise I'll be looking like a beached whale in my bikini!

5th August

Dear Suz,

Well, honey, I'm here in sunny Spain and I'm feeling a mixture of nervous fear and excitement. Everywhere I go people are speaking a foreign language, which I guess isn't too surprising but it's so strange. My flat – or 'el flato' – as my mum is calling it – is small but cozy. Actually it's more than cozy, it's bloody boiling at the moment and I'm sweating like a trooper. First thing tomorrow I'm going to buy a fan, an electric one, however I might also get a Spanish one as I'm now living in Spain!

It still feels like I'm just on holiday, especially as I'm not working at the moment but I'm sure it will hit home once my boxes arrive. I wouldn't say I'm a materialistic person but I so want my things around me so I can set up home and get the place looking like someone actually lives here. This morning I said 'hola' to my neighbour, an old Spanish lady. She smiled and said something to me, which I didn't understand at all so I just nodded and smiled back. I'm sure I'll start to pick up the lingo soon enough but now I wish I had taken Spanish GCSE instead of French! (not that I actually passed my French

GCSE!)

Hey Suz, I've decided to make a couple of changes to my life now I've made the big move and the biggest one is to cut out Facebook, Twitter and even Email if I can help it. It's just that over the last few years I've found myself almost permanently attached to them, as if they were ruling my life for me and I just don't want that any more. I'd end up receiving 50 emails a day from work, companies, recruitment agencies and so on and I want to be free from that. Social Media also feels like it's become a place for people to look at you, judge you, and never actually be social with you. Instead, I'm proposing writing letters to one another. I can already see you rolling your eyes but I just think, it will do me the world of good. Anyway, who doesn't love receiving a letter in the post? Please say you'll give it a go and spread the word. If you do, I'll let you come over and stay in my small sweaty flat and you can share my fan with me!

Lots of love,

Rach xxx

P.S: Can you pop in on Mum and Dad and see how they are? I'm sure they are fine but just in case they need anything.

10th August

Dear Rachel,

Dinner at 10pm! You must get terrible indigestion at that time of night. Your Father says make sure you don't drink the tap water. He said when he was in Spain in 1978 he had the most terrible tummy for about a week. Wouldn't want you to suffer like that!

Anyway, enough of that talk; how's life with more than 4 sets of clothes? Bet you're proud of your old Mummy. I sorted them out well and truly. At first they ran off a load of excuses and even said they had delivered the boxes three weeks ago. I told them that would have been good service seeing that you only moved there less than two weeks ago!

How does the 'el flato' look now that you've got all your bits and bobs? I'm sure it will be lovely and homely soon enough. Talking of home, I popped down Greenfields in the village yesterday, and ordered some new fabric for your curtains. Hate the thought of you having vile curtains. My mother always taught me to judge a woman by the standard of her window dressing. Don't want your visitors thinking badly of you now do we? They should arrive in the next week or so. I've added a special large stamp to the parcel and 5 first class stamps especially for you!

That reminds me; I bumped into that funny woman from the local Am Drams and she sent her love. Can't think of her name but she's the one that we always called 'The Cloud' because her hair looked like it was about to fly off!

9

Talking of flying off, I better do the same. Your father wants to take me out to the local DIY store! Who says romance is dead!

Oh that reminds me. I made a bit of a faux pas this week. Old Mrs. Bloomsbury died last week so I sent Miss Bloomsbury Junior a sympathy card and said how sad I was and that your father and I were thinking of her at this tragic time. I then ended the card with LOL Penny and Derek. You never told me 'LOL' actually meant 'laugh out loud'! I thought it was short for lots of love! Heavens knows what she thought!

Love, peace and happiness,

Mum and Dad xxx

11ᵗʰ August

Dear Rach,

You sangria-soaked hussy! How are you? Already missing you so much! Can I book my flight out to see you yet?

Loving the pics of the flat. Looks well lush; compact - but so are you, so that's a good match. I've already spotted my sunbathing spot on the terrace! I'm looking so pasty at the moment. I'm so in need of a spot of vitamin D!

Loving this letter writing idea. When your letter came through the post I thought it was a belated Valentine's card from that hunk from the gym that does the body pump class. He could pump my body any day of the week! Anyway enough of the smut and back to this letter idea. I love it, I didn't even roll my eyes. I love it so much in fact I've especially popped to WHSmiths and bought a card selection five-bloody-ninetynine for 8 pieces of card with baby animals on them!) but at least I'm stocked up for the next few weeks. We will still chat on the phone and text, though, won't we? You're not going full no-techno on me like your Mother, are you? Has she learnt how to change channels yet?

Talking of your Mum I popped round there the other day to

see how they were and arrived whilst your Mum was on the phone having a very interesting conversation! I didn't mean to ear wig but I'm glad I did: listen to this. Your Mum was explaining to the person on the other end of the phone that your delivery hadn't arrived and that the packages were only small and that she'd inspected them herself before they had been sent off. Then she went very quiet, then very red. Then she quickly made her apologies and hung up. Apparently instead of calling 'The Big Parcel Company' she had phoned up the male stripper dance group called 'The Big Packages!' The look on her face! Classic!

Anyway must dash, I've got a body pump class to attend!

Love Suz x

P.S: So did anything happen with Marcus? He was so wanting to give you a goodbye snog. That man is too good-looking for his own good!

16th August

Dear Mum and Dad,

My 'el flato' is looking much more homely now that all my bits and bobs have turned up. Only 2 weeks late! You must have sorted those 'Big Package' boys out good and proper! Did you have to go down and inspect the packages yourself or were they already in safe hands?!

The material for the curtains arrived too. It's gorgeous, mum, it certainly gives the room a touch of 'English charm'. I've not seen the Union Jack look so good since Geri Halliwell wore it as a miniskirt to the Brit awards! Oh yes, and talking of miniskirts, I've been able to wear mine again now that I've unpacked all the boxes containing my clothes. I can't believe I've got so many shoes and that's even after suffering the pains of doing a car-boot sale before I left! The weather here is gorgeous so it's short shorts and vest tops most days; however, after eating dinners at both 7pm and 10pm, my short shorts won't hold in my fat arse for much longer!

The city of Barcelona is amazing, Mum. I've spent a few days exploring and have decided that my part of town, el Raval, is what you would call 'lived in';

whilst not the prettiest part of Barcelona, it is certainly the most colourful. There are shops and bars and all manner of people living down my street. Certainly a change from village life and as Dad always says: 'change does you good'.

I'm certainly hoping it does because in a month a whole lot of change is coming my way! I start my new job on the first Monday in October and, to tell the truth, I'm a bit terrified - but I keep telling myself it can't be as bad as working with Victoria! They're first sending me on a 4 week beginner's Spanish course though so at least I'll know the basics for when I start. In the meantime I'm going to look for a handy man to help me put up the new curtains and sort out a few other jobs in the 'el flato'. The tap in the bathroom currently has a nasty habit of spraying out water all over me, giving the effect that I've peed myself. Not a good look, I can tell you!

Lots of love,

Rachel xxx

P.S If you bump into the Cloud woman again, Felicity, send her my love and tell her to return my leggings she borrowed from me when she performed in Fame. You never know when a pair of glow-in-the-dark pink leggings will come in handy!.

21st August

Dear Rachel,

I can't believe that Suzy told you about my phone call. That naughty girl, I knew she wouldn't be able to keep it quiet. On the plus side, I received an invitation to see the Big Packages perform live on stage this weekend! Apparently the man on the other end of the phone found the whole conversation rather amusing so sent me two free tickets. I don't suspect your Father will want to go so I'll take Suzy instead!

The weather here really is dreadful at the moment so keep your 'it's-so-hot-and-sunny' comments to yourself, if you don't mind. My geraniums have lost all their petals and your father's sunflower has drooped. We had planned on going for a picnic on the beach but the weather put the kibosh on that one so ended up sitting in the car on Worthing Seafront, eating our ham sandwiches and sharing a packet of Frazzles. Still, it got your Father out and I have to say sitting inside a steamy-windowed car brought back a few memories. Oh, how we laughed!

Looking forward to seeing a photo of the new curtains up. Make sure you sing the National Anthem as they are raised! LOL (See - I can use 'LOL' correctly now!) Your Father says only hire someone who knows what they're doing. Quite why he feels he's able to give advice on DIY is beyond me, though, every time he attempts it, the outcome falls far short of the desired result! At this point in time I will list his top three DIY disasters:

1.The wallpapering of the bedroom in 1972 (our first home), when he had wallpapered the entire room with the pattern upside down! It wouldn't have mattered so much if it had just been an abstract pattern but seeing as it was exotic birds, every morning I woke up for 2 years, I thought I was going to fall out of a tree!

2. Then we had the classic chandelier disaster of 1985, when he brought a crystal chandelier the size of a small car and expected it to hang in the living room. Well, seeing as we weren't living in Buckingham Palace at the time, it didn't come as a great surprise when it filled the entire room. It was so big we had to walk around it to get from one side of the room to the other. Hence it only stayed up 3 days.

3. Finally we had the grand disaster of Christmas 2002 when the IKEA table Father put together (no, he didn't read the instructions) collapsed mid-dinner, covering Grandma with cranberry sauce and Brussels sprouts!

So, darling, I hope your DIY experiences go more smoothly than those of your father! Have a good week.

Love, peace and happiness,

Mum and Dad xxx

24th August

Dear Rachel,

Who knew your Mum was such a naughty girl?! The Big Package boys released her inner tiger! Grrrrrrr! At the beginning of the night she sat nervously sipping her Cinzano and lemonade as the boys strutted their stuff (and mighty good stuff it was too!) but by the end of the night she was shoving 50p coins down Truncheon Trevor's posing pouch. Your mum's a right laugh when she gets going, I can certainly see where you get it from!

Now, on to matters more pressing, (I kind of feel like a modern day Elizabeth Bennet when I'm writing to you. I should most certainly start wearing a bonnet and one of those tight corsets to show off my plump bosoms!) Yesterday, after copping an eyeful of Fireman Sam's hose, I went to the Anchor for a drink with some of the girls and whom did I see but Marcus Flynn. Well, Mr. Flynn was looking as gorgeous as ever, with his tousled blond hair and smouldering looks and that big broad chest... (etc, etc..) when he came over to talk to me. And even though I was dressed in my finest low cut top he didn't even start with the pleasantries, and instead he went straight in with "How's Rachel? How's she settling in? Have you heard how's she's getting on? Did I have your contact details? Blah, blah, blah!"

I tell you what, Rach, he was pining for you like a great big sexy dog. I still don't know how you two didn't get together. You would have been like Brad Pitt and Jennifer Aniston, the perfect couple! Anyway, I told him you were doing this letter writing 'thing' and passed him on your address, I'm not convinced he's the writing type but wait and see. Soon you might be receiving manly-scented letters in the post!

Right that's enough from me for today. I need to head off to the gym for a session of Body Combat. I've discovered that the spunky Body Pump instructor also does Body Combat classes so I'm hoping to have some close proximity training with him very soon!

Love and hugs,

Suz x

29th August

Dear Suz, (aka Elizabeth Bennet)

So did you get your claws into Mr. Body Pump/Combat? All the dirty details in a plain brown envelope soon please!

I'm so glad you're writing to me telling me all the gossip. I have to say I check my post box every day with excitement and if there's a letter there it absolutely makes my day. If not, I sulk as I walk back up the seven flights of stairs back up to my 'el flato'. There is a lift but it's so old and rickety I'm scared that I'll be trapped in it so at the moment it's the 72 steps for me. (At least my arse will look amazing this time next year! No more terrible aerobics DVD's for me!) Anyway back to letters - I think I'm going to start a campaign to bring back letter writing. It's such a therapeutic thing to do. I usually sit on my little balcony at my little table and if I time it right, bathe in the sunlight as I write to you and mum. (I guess if I'm going to start campaigning for more letter writing I should perhaps extend my writing circle. Especially as one Marcus Flynn hasn't graced my letterbox with his best wishes!)

As for your news from the Anchor, well, my answer

to that would be that Marcus Flynn had his chance and he missed it. I was his for the taking at Miss Elaine's Christmas party last year and just as we were about to kiss under the mistletoe along trotted Lucinda Long-Legs and snatched him away from me. Not that I feel bitter - (I don't want to turn out like Victoria Plum after all) - but he was all I dreamed about for two whole years and then when things looked like they were finally going to happen he was whisked away by the girl with the longest legs in the entire world! And now that she's flown back off to New York he's suddenly realizing what he missed out on. Me!! And whilst I may not have legs the length of a giraffe and the body of Kate Moss, I am a catch and many a man would be proud to call me his woman. Anyway I have now successfully set up home here in Barcelona (curtains still not up but 'el flato' is certainly looking rather homely) and I have moved on from Marcus Flynn in more ways than one!

Ooooh, that felt good to get off my chest. I told you writing is good for you. I would have told all that to my neighbour but she's about 100 and doesn't speak any English. She still manages to beat me up the seven flights of stairs, though! These old Spanish women are tough old birds. Must be all the olives they eat!

Talking of food. I've discovered the most amazing ice-cream shop in Barceloneta (used to be the old fishing part of the city but is now where all the tourists go to the beach - me included!) They do a banana split ice-cream with real shards of chocolate in it and it's divine! If I wasn't so worried about looking like a fat cow I'd go there every day! When you visit I'll take you and force you to have one, I know these days you're the keep-fit queen but even you must have a day off. Anyway, I thought all Australians loved ice-cream?

Tomorrow I start my beginners' Spanish course!!! I'm half excited but in equal parts shitting myself as I've not actually done any studying since doing my A Levels at St. Joseph's. And even then it wasn't languages; do you remember doing art together with bonkers Mrs. Thingy?? (can't remember her name?) That day she brought in a piece of bark for us to draw as she thought it's linear qualities were most erotic! Ewww! Lol I remember you taking one look at it and throwing it out the window. I haven't actually studied a language since I was 15 and that was French and I was terrible! I seem to remember studying it for 5 long years and still only learning colours, foods and the phrase 'Voulez vous coucher avec moi ce soir'. And that's only because of watching Moulin Rouge 20 times with you on a Saturday night! So I'll let you know how it goes but expect mucho embarrassmento!

Miss you, Suz, let's book you in for a visit? Over New Year or will you be back Down Under with the folks?

Lots of love,

Rach xxx

P.S As for being a chip off the old block I certainly am. You didn't happen to take any photos of Mum popping sop's down P.C Plod's thong did you?! Would love to see the look on my Dad's face if he knew what she had got up to! Hee, hee!

29th August

Dear Rachel,

I'm not sure what that naughty Suzy has told you but I must say I found the whole strip show terribly common. You should have seen the way women were throwing themselves at those oiled-up Greek Gods. I certainly won't be returning to that den of sin (well, not until they return anyway!) Oh, how we laughed; I can see why you're friends with Suzy, she's such a fun girl. Mind you I did have to remind her about her language at times, made me blush at the vocabulary she uses. Must be her Australian roots, having said that I've never heard them swear on Neighbours or Home and Away. The occasional 'rack off' but nothing like the unladylike words she was using. Apart from that though we had a wonderful time. Just don't tell your Father. I told him we had gone to a flower arranging show!

Talking of flower arranging, you'll be very proud of your Mummy as she's just been voted as new Madam Chairwoman for the upcoming year! It was apparently a close run thing though as I was up against Penelope Godleming and she had all the old farts that have been members for the last 100 years supporting her but the outgoing Chairwoman, Veronica Vase (ridiculous name!) put in a good word for me with the women from the W.I and that swung it my way. So now I'm Madam Chairwoman and my first act will be to finally get the tea ladies to buy in some decent coffee and the odd packet of chocolate Hobnobs. That should go down well and get some of the old biddies on side. After that I plan to organize a trip to the Chelsea Flower Show next year. A bit of fun is certainly needed to cheer them all up, I say!

Your Father sends his love. He's gone down the Charity Shop to see if he can find a bargain. I'm already dreading what he might bring back, though, as last time he brought back all the crap I had sent down there the week before. You know that ugly old statue of a dancing clown with balloons his mother gave us on our wedding day? Well I bagged that up and gave it to good old Oxfam, only for him to return home a day later announcing that he had found me another of the same statue. Natural, I hadn't told him that it was the same hideous thing I had just got rid of so now he thinks we have a matching pair! Men! What are they like!

Have you started your Spanish course yet? I couldn't remember when you said you were starting. I hope it's not too challenging, though I'm sure you'll pick it up quickly, especially as you're living there. I bet when your Father and I visit (In May or June?) you'll be fluent, which would be a good thing as it would stop your Father using the usual Brit abroad method which involves speaking loudly and slowly whilst waving your arms about a lot. Highly embarrassing for all concerned, really! I'll never forget the time when we were in Greece and he tried to order the chicken by flapping his arms around like wings. The waiter thought he was having a fit and tried to call the ambulance! He never got his chicken. Think he had to make do with some sort of meat covered in feta.

Now I hate to use the 'c' word this early in the year but what are your plans for Christmas, darling? I know you've only been gone a month but if you're coming home for Christmas it's probably best you book your flights now to save yourself a euro or two. It will also give your Great Aunt Shelly plenty of time to start knitting your Christmas gift. She said that if you were coming home for Christmas she'd knit you a patterned skirt (don't ask me!) but if you weren't coming back she'd have to send something in the post so would have to make something parcel-shaped! Again, I have no idea what that could be, a tea cozy perhaps, so, anyway, just let me know what you decide to do and I'll pass on your answer.

By the way, your Father's just returned as we speak and he's done it once again! I smuggled three of his most revolting jumpers out the house a month ago and took them to that Charity Shop at the top of the village - where no one ever goes in because it smells of cat's pee - and he's just walked in the kitchen proudly showing me two of the very same jumpers that he bought as a bargain! I can't win!

Love, peace and happiness,

Mum and Dad xxx

P.S: The Great British Bake Off is fantastic this year. Every year it gets better and better and Mel and Sue just make it for me. I'm also partial to a bit of Paul Hollywood too, why, he's a silver fox! Have you done any baking yet, darling, or is it too hot? I bumped into Gill (Mrs. Ashley) yesterday and she asked the same thing. Such a nice woman, she was your best teacher by far. She's also watching Bake Off and said that you might be able to catch it on Youtube or iPlayer, whatever those are.

Chapter 2
September - All Things New

1ˢᵗ September

Dear Mum and Dad,

Well, September has arrived and I've joined a gym, started my Spanish course and my Bicing Card has arrived! One thing at a time though!

1. Now that I've finally sorted out all my paperwork (The Spanish do love their paperwork!) I have been able to join a gym. My reckoning is that because the weather here is so gorgeous pretty much all the time, I'm going to be on the beach for maybe 99% of the year (ok, maybe not as much as that, but a lot!) so I'm going to need a beach body. At present, however, instead of having a nice flat tummy and a toned physique, I actually have a muffin top and bingo wings!!! As a result of this I have therefore joined the 'el gymo' where I will be swimming, cycling, rowing and maybe even body-pumping my way to the perfect summer body. I'll keep you posted!

2. It was back to school for me this week as I started my Spanish course and, boy, was it difficult! I felt like I was in a whirlwind of words. Even though I felt way out of my comfort zone, I have to say I also loved it as I felt I was starting on my Spanish learning

journey. So far my journey consists of 'Hola, gracias, gazpacho and adios' but at least it's a start. My fellow classmates are all very nice apart from one know-it-all girl who I suspect is actually Spanish and just likes being a right old show off!

3. You'll be pleased to know that the saying 'you never forget how to ride a bike' is true. I may have not ridden on a bike since I was 9 years old but I've not forgotten how. Here in Barcelona, you see, we have a bike card, which means you can use a bike for up to half an hour and pootle round the city going from A to B. It's really handy, especially as you get to see so much more of the city. It's rather fun too. When riding down a hill yesterday I couldn't resist lifting my legs and letting out a big Wheeeee! (Of the vocal kind, that is!)

How are you and Dad? All good I hope. I hope he's behaving himself! Are you planning anything nice for your birthday this month? I'm sorry I won't be there to celebrate, seems odd not being around for your special day; however, I'm sure you'll have a great time, especially if Great Aunt Shelly knits you a rainbow waistcoat like she did last year!! I guess you'll be wearing that on your big day won't you? Hee, hee!

Would love to write more but I'm afraid the beach is calling me for a relaxing afternoon, lazing in the sun. Yes we have sun in September too! England needs to seriously take note of the Spanish weather.

Hugs and kisses,

Rachel xxx

3rd September

Darling Rachel,

How the devil are you? I bet you're having an absolutely fabulous time in Espana! Everyone at the Latchington Dramatic Society sends their love and is missing you greatly. I more so than all the others because I'm directing this season's pantomime. 'Cinderella', and you would have made the most wonderful Prince Charming. Instead I'm probably going to be stuck with 'Fat Janet' and you just can't have an overweight principal boy as the thigh slap jiggles on for far too long; but if it's between her and Daisy Carter, who can't even remember her own name, let alone her lines, I think Fat Janet will have to do! Naturally, Felicity will play the Fairy Godmother as her diction is perfect and as her natural hair-do is so big we won't need to buy her a wig. She sends her love, by the way, and says she's still got your luminous pink leggings and she'll pop them round to your mum's house.

Talking of your mum, I spotted her in the village a few weeks ago but she was in a hurry, carrying a large quantity of Union Jack material so I didn't get the chance to chat to her. I guess she must have been making some sort of fancy dress costume or novelty item with all that garish material! I'll pop round for a cup of tea next week and, no doubt, will find out all about it. Actually I've just had a wonderful thought. If she has any material left after her creation I'll use it for a couple of ghastly ugly sister gowns for the Ball scene! Hee, hee!

How's life in Barcelona, then? Bet it's a step away from life in little old Latchington! I'm so proud of you for doing it, though. I spent 2 years traveling the world when I was your age and loved every minute of it. Went surfing on the Gold Coast in Oz,

31

parachuting off Table Mountain in South Africa, tap danced on a bar in New York and even had dinner with a Maharaja in India. He had the most wonderful marble palace close to Delhi; he wanted me to stay and be his wife but I was dating Rodney, the usher at the Dome Cinema in Worthing, at the time and he could get me in free to see all my favourite films, so I politely declined. I'm sure you'll have some wonderful tales of your own very soon and I'll want to hear them all.

Stay in touch, darling, and think of me this week as I try desperately to cast Cinderella. One thing's for certain, I won't be casting Karen Crickmoore again, not after she fell off stage last year and landed in the vicar's lap!

Much love,

Miss Elaine xx

P.S: Love writing a letter so will definitely write again. Never been one for sitting at a computer for hours on end, anyway.

4th September

Dear Rach,

Just a quick one as I've got a busy week at work, we've got important potential new clients we're pitching our ad campaign to visiting and I'm leading the pitch! Bloody hell!!! So this week I'm going to be all professional and business woman-like. Kind of like Melanie Griffiths (pre puffy lips) in Working Girl – 'I have a head for business and a body for sin'. Hee, hee!

Glad you let off steam concerning a certain man I shall not name for he is of no consequence. (said like Elizabeth Bennet) I believe that your future love lies in Barcelona anyway. Spanish men are well spunky so get your fat ice-cream munching arse out there and find yourself a lovely bronzed lollypop to suck on! (Elizabeth Bennet didn't say that bit!)

How are things with the love life, anyway? How come I've not heard you mention any sexy Spanish men yet? I thought you'd be surrounded by them by now! I was picturing you in a kind of Spanish version of Shirley Valentine!

Got to dash, need to practice my presentation by watching Working Girl.

Miss you, darl,

Suz x

P.S: Still working on Mr. Body Pump aka Jason. At the moment I've got competition in the shape of 'Barbie Sunshine' a plastic looking 20 year old who has just joined the class. Don't worry, though, honey, I always get my man!

5th September

Dear Rachel,

Well, my dear it's been a busy and eventful old week for your dear mother. I can honestly say I have not stopped, unlike your Father, who's spent most of the week with his feet up snoozing on the sofa. (Lazy old fart!) I, however, have been a busy girl so shall run you through my weekly goings on.

Monday: I started the week by deciding to blitz the garden. Summer (all 2 weeks of it!) is sadly over for us poor unfortunate souls in the UK and so the garden needed putting to bed for the winter. What with all the rain we've had it was like a jungle! So I spent the whole day digging up the main flower bed, cutting back that damned pampas grass (really I don't see the point in such a vile plant!), mowing the lawn and finally picking the last of the runner beans. All was going swimmingly until the postman entered the garden whilst I was picking some of the apples from the tree in the back garden; trouble was, I didn't see or hear him until he was right up beside me causing me to scream with shock, then fall off the ladder into the freshly laid compost. I was absolutely covered! Looked like the monster from the black lagoon. The postman kindly helped me up and apologised profusely for startling me, then handed me your latest letter which made me smile, even though I was covered in poo!

Tuesday: Went into the village to do the weekly shop and was rather pleased to see that my favourite biscuits had a BOGOF (Buy one get one free) offer on them. You know how I love a bargain! I do not, however, like the new owners of the stationery shop at the top of the village. I just went in there to get a pack of envelopes and the woman, a mean looking thing, followed me round the shop as if I were a shoplifter! Bloody cheek! Every time I looked up she was there, lurking round the corner like an undercover agent. What did she think I was going to do, shove a packet of biros and a bag of elastic bands up my jumper? I certainly won't be returning there. She got an evil look as I left the shop and I left the door open too! Showed her!

Then later that night I stayed in and watched the Great British Bake Off in peace because your father was at his photography club. (More of that later!!!) This series must be the best yet. Last night they were baking muffins, your favourites! Have you managed to watch it yet? It's the final soon and I've arranged a little party with Gill and Miss Elaine coming over to watch it with me. We are each going to bake our own cake or pastry to share but I know Gill's will be ten times better than mine. There's no chance of beating a Home Economics teacher at her own game, after all!

Wednesday: Started the day with a quick hoover and a dust around then prepared for my first official Flower Club session as Madam Chairwoman! And what a session it was too! The visiting flower arranger was marvelous. A very flamboyant man called Francis who specialized in arrangements with a movie theme. Each theme was beautifully matched with music from the film and a story linked to each movie. He created 5 different centrepieces, each one more original than the previous: Star Wars was a stunning blend of dark foliage with splashes of stargazer lilies and a most ingenious use of Christmas lights in an old Pringles tube covered in tinfoil. Titanic was represented with a red carnation wreath creation which paid homage to the victims, whilst also serving as a dinner-party talking point. Mission Impossible started well with a vase of sunflowers balanced on a Japanese sacred stone but, sadly, he got a bit carried away with the speed of the music and the whole arrangement fell off the stage and landed near Mrs. Bartholomew's Zimmer frame. Thankfully, she saw the funny side and everyone laughed! He then finished with Pricilla, Queen of the Desert, which was a glorious display of gladioli and eucalyptus leaves in a giant silver high heel (I think your friend Rory may have liked that one). The whole afternoon was a real success and I even won a packet of jammy biscuits on the raffle!

Thursday: After being inspired by the Bake Off and after going to the trouble of harvesting some apples from the tree I decided to bake a blackberry and apple pie! One of your favourites, I know! If I could have posted you a slice I certainly would have done, as it was a very good bake. No soggy bottom for me! Unfortunately, later that afternoon as I was tucking into a jammy biscuit one of my fillings decided to come out. Grrr! My raffle win wasn't so good after all.

Friday: Most people hate the dentist but I have to say I rather enjoy going. I know it sounds strange - but not everyone has Dr. Parker. Rachel, he's the most handsome dentist you are ever likely to meet. It's such a shame you're not in the village any more as he would certainly have made a fine boyfriend for you. I might recommend him to Suzy - but only if she cuts down on the *swearing.*

My visit to see Dr. Parker left me a little embarrassed, however, and rather angry with your Father. For, unknown to me, Dr. Parker belongs to your father's camera club and also unknown to me, your Father decided to take along a topless photo of me, taken during a family holiday to Ibiza in the 1980's, when I looked like Princess Diana. The theme that week was 'look-alikes' and, whilst Dr. Parker took along a picture of his Spaniel, who apparently looks like Cher, your father presented the photo of me. My temper and embarrassment quickly subsided, however, as Dr. Parker said the photo was greeted with universal acclaim for its portrait of a timeless beauty! Your Father was still given a good telling off but I had to praise him for his excellent photography skills.

Saturday: After the topless photo mishap, your Father felt guilty so took me to Jane Austen's Cottage for the day to make up for it. What a gorgeous house she lived in with her family. We were up at the crack of dawn so managed to look around without too many other people getting in our way. At one point I was in her writing room all alone and I felt quite emotional. To be that close to where Mr. Darcy and Miss. Bennet were created gave me goose pimples! I've enclosed a few photos of us in the garden holding a copy of Pride and Prejudice.

Following that we had a cream tea in a nearby café and even though the dentist told me to go easy with my new filling, I still scoffed the scone down with a generous helping of raspberry jam on top! You only live once so enjoy it I say! Having said that, though, the scones were no match for yours, darling. You always did manage to bake the biggest scones I've ever seen.

Sunday: Today I've not actually done much except write you this letter and once I get your Father to run it down the post box, I shall join him on the sofa and we will be two lazy old farts together!

Hope all is well with you my love. How's the Spanish going? Fluent yet?! Are my curtains up yet? Your Father and I want to see photos so pop them on the interweb so next time Suzy comes over we can see them on her laptop.

Love, peace and happiness,

Mum and Dad xxx

8th September

Dear Miss Elaine,

So lovely to hear from you and how I wish I could don my fishnet tights and slap my thigh for you this Christmas as your preferred Prince Charming. However I am quite frankly having far too much fun here in Barcelona!

Miss Elaine, you would simply love it here too and I demand you visit me once you have finished directing what will be known as the pantomime of the year! I can't guarantee finding you an Indian Prince but I can guarantee a jug of sangria, a plateful of delicious tapas and a dance with some hot chicos in the local salsa bar!

Last month I went to the fiestas in an area of the city called Gracia and had the best time. About 20 streets in the barrio (neighbourhood) decorate their particular street with a theme and really go to town on it. Imagine Sherwood Avenue in the village being totally transformed into Jurassic Park, complete with papier-mâché dinosaurs and lampposts disguised as palm trees. They don't stop there, however, as every street has music playing, stages with performers or

DJ's on them and there are bars or tables set up everywhere to sell mojitos. It's just incredible! I went round with one of the girls from my Spanish class, called Lucy. A lovely girl, originally from London, who now lives here with her boyfriend. We had a fantastic night and the best part of it is that all the community gets involved and uses recycled materials to make everything. You should come next year as you'd get loads of ideas for pantomime sets! Good luck with the panto, by the way. I'm sure it will all work out fine. I'll try and convince my friend Suz to come down to the auditions. I'm not really sure she can act (not that half the members of the society can either) but she's got a cracking pair of legs and would look amazing in a pair of fishnets! Write again soon, I want regular Cinderella updates!

Lots of love,

Rachel xxx

P.S The Ugly Sister's Union Jack dresses are hanging up in my lounge! Mum sent the 'fancy dress' material to me for curtains so, unfortunately, you'll have to look elsewhere for ghastly material for their ball gowns!

10th September

Dear Suz,

Well, Melanie Griffiths, how did the BIG presentation go? I'm sure you blew them away with your über-professional presenting style and top-quality sales pitch. When do you find out if the clients liked it?

As for me, I have been busy preparing for my future employment by continuing with my Spanish classes but if my terrible Spanish is anything to go by, my future career looks stuffed! It's so hard, Suz, I can't help feeling like a right old dummy; whenever they ask me anything, my mind just goes blank. I'm sure they all think I'm a total idiot. I have, however, mastered food and drink and, to tell the truth, that is, in fact, one of the most important parts of learning any language. I now just need to master the other one billion aspects!

On a cheerier note, it turns out that my local handyman is a very sexy Spanish dish! As you know, Mum sent me reams of Great British fabric to dress my windows with so I needed someone skilled to hang the curtain pole for me as well as complete a few other jobs around the house. However, things never quite go to plan, do they? So just before Alberto arrived ("Alberto".... - I like to say the name over and over as it has a lovely sound to it!), I went into the bathroom to wash my hands and the dodgy tap sprayed water all over my crotch area. Then as I was desperately towelling myself down he came in, because I had left the front door open to get a breeze running through. So there I am looking like I've just peed myself and in walks the most handsome man I think I've ever seen in my life! I tried desperately to explain, in absolutely terrible Spanish and using hand gestures, that I hadn't actually weed myself and that it was in fact the dodgy 'el tapo' that I needed him to 'el fixo'. He simply smiled so I briskly moved him through to the lounge, where I yet again used actions and Spanglish to explain that, even though it wasn't my choice of material, I did indeed want the British Flag raised as curtains in the lounge. At that point the cheeky bugger said, in perfect English:" Should we sing the National Anthem now or after they've been hung?"

Oh Suz, I almost died of embarrassment but he was very kind and said that I had actually used three correct words in my visual explanation and that was a good start. That's when I decided that Alberto (Alberto, Alberto, Alberto!) wasn't merely a pretty

43

face, he was also rather sweet.

After that I made him a cup of tea; he lived in London for 5 years so was partial to a cuppa, and gave him a piece of my home baked coffee cake, which he said tasted amazing, then he got to work. And what a marvelous job he did, too! In next to no time he erected the pole (Ooo Matron!) and fixed the dodgy tap. Then, just before he left we did indeed sing a quick verse of 'God Save The Queen' and I pulled the Union Jack curtains as a sign of respect to dear Queen Elizabeth.

Sadly, after that he had to go as he had another job to do but he did give me his card and said that if I needed anything else fixing he'd be happy to pop around and mend it for me. As you can imagine, I am currently trying to break as many things around the flat as I can just so that Alberto returns post-haste. I have also decided that next time he needs to fix something I'll put the heating up full blast so that he needs to remove his top whilst he's working! By the way, talking of removing clothing, how's it going with Body Pump Jason? Any closer to getting a one to one session or has Barbie Sunshine put a halt to those plans?!

Love and kisses, chica,

Rachel xxx

P.S: I can't believe I have Union Jack curtains in my flat! I fear I'm turning into my mother!

15th September

Dear Rach,
Alberto the carpenter sounds like a total hottie! If I were you I'd get a sledgehammer right now and trash the place. Then turn the heating up full and dial his number for an emergency session!

Presentation was a total disaster. I got all flustered and forgot what I was going to say and generally cocked it right up. At one point I managed to spill my glass of water all over the meeting-room table and all because the man I was pitching to was bloody gorgeous and a terrible distraction. However, I managed to save the day and win the pitch by shagging him later that evening!!! Terrible, I know. I can already see you rolling your eyes and tutting like your mother does. In my defence, though, he was the one who flirted with me first and asked me out for dinner to discuss the pitch further. I was just trying to do my job in a professional manner - and then I accidently slept with him. Mind you, he was obviously impressed with my 'evening performance', as the next day his company commissioned us to do their advertising for them! My boss couldn't believe it, should have seen the look on the grumpy git's face. Needless to say since then I've been treated as employee of the month, much to everyone's surprise, especially moody Karen with the ponytail, who took great glee in the fact that I cocked up the presentation. She and the others have - naturally - not been told I slept with Mr. Stevens, as that would kind of ruin things.

Anyhow, with my work life now flourishing and possibly my love life too, for that matter, (if Mr. Sexy Steven's wants to pursue things further) all is good with the world.

Oh, by the way Rory sends his love. He promises to write soon and apologizes for not writing so far but he's got a new puppy and it seems to have taken over his life. I wouldn't hold your breath expecting a letter from him but I do know he misses you terribly and that he will be visiting with me in the spring. His puppy is a total cutie and so far they are inseparable; but I also know what Rory's like with the latest fads. In January, he had to have the latest mobile, then a month later dropped it down the loo. In March he took up knitting because of that knitting program on BBC2 but after knitting half a scarf gave all the kit to your Mum to pass onto your Great Auntie Shelly. Then there was the kite-surfing but after almost being dragged across the English Channel and needing to be rescued by the Lifeboat, he decided to get a dog. So for the time being 'Mr. Paws' is the new fad. I just hope, for the dog's sake, he doesn't get dropped down the loo - or given to Great Auntie Shelly, for that matter!

Hugs and kisses you old trollop,

Suz x

P.S Do you like the new set of arty-farty cards I bought? This one is from Picasso's blue period, I do believe! Pop it in a frame and you'd never know the difference between the real thing and a WHSmiths greetings card!

16th September

Dear Rachel,

Lovely chatting to you on the phone last week, darling; how your old mum misses you. I know you've only been away less than a couple of months but since we used to see each other every week it just seems a long time. I was so happy, however, to hear all your news and to hear you sounding so content and happy in your new life. I like the sound of your old neighbour, she seems like a lively old bird! I'm imagining a Spanish version of our neighbor, dear old Joyce. I went round to see how she was the other day and found her in the garden reminiscing about how the garden used to look and the birds that once visited it. Couldn't help laughing though when she told me how she used to have tits front and back! I'm presuming she meant blue tits! Hee, hee! Can you believe she's lived there for 60 years! The garden's looking a bit wild these days so I'm sending your father round there this week to try and knock it back into shape. Will certainly do him some good and will give me 5 mins peace and quiet too!

Talking of your father, his latest photographic assignment is the human body! Apparently after my 'photo feature' last month the members (all 12 of the dirty old buggers) decided to have a monthly focus on the human form and in tonight's session they have a naked model to photograph! Never seen your father leave the house so quickly. Really, it's quite disturbing, some poor girl sat in front of 12 David Bailey wannabes while they all attach their zoom lenses and take pictures of her chest. I told Suzy and she said she thought it was the new barmaid who was posing.

Calls her Barbie Sunshine, don't think that's her real name, mind you.

Changing the subject, I had a strange conversation with Miss Elaine about material for the 'Ugly Sisters' ball gowns. She seemed to think she saw me with fancy dress material or something. Anyway wasn't quite sure what she meant but by the end of the conversation, I had somehow been talked into to helping backstage with the costume team for the Am Dram pantomime. Tried to convince Suzy to take part but she says she's away in Australia over the Christmas holidays. Your other friend, Rory, has got a part, though. He's playing one of the step-sisters alongside the local fireman, Rob. They should make a pretty pair, opposites in every possible way!

The Great British Bake Off Final was wonderful. So glad you've been able to watch it! I won't say who won but let's just say it was not who you'd expect! Miss Elaine and Gill thoroughly enjoyed it too and I'm pleased to say all three of us produced lovely cakes. My sponge was a tad on the dry side, I have to say, and Miss Elaine's did have a slightly soggy bottom but Gill's was perfection. We all went home with a doggy-bag of cakes and if your father is well behaved tomorrow he can have some as a reward!

Love, peace and happiness,

Mum and Dad xxx

P.S: You'll never guess what! Your father's just come home from Camera Club looking rather disappointed, as the naked model wasn't in fact the busty barmaid but in fact old Cyril Wheatly, who's in his 80's! That showed them!

18th September

Dear Rach,
So sorry I've not written before but you know me I'm much more a Facebook/Twitter kind of guy. Mr. Paws, my brand gorgeous new sausage dog has been taking up all of my time. He's absolutely beautiful but it's like having a baby. I'm rushed off my feet with feeding him, taking him for walks and generally spoiling him rotten. I will make more of an effort in future, though, and I have to say I enjoyed picking out this postcard. Which sexy surfer is your fav. then? I chose the big buff one on the end. Talking of big and buff guess who I'm ugly sister with in the panto! Rob the fireman!! Yummy! I'm already looking forward to sharing the changing rooms with him!

Been chatting with Suz about visiting and we've decided on February. I was checking online and it says there's a great carnival on in Sitges (not too far from Barcelona is it?) and was thinking that the three of us would make gorgeous carnival queens!

Will write again soon as long as you promise to come and see the panto in December. You cannot miss it, Fat Janet is playing the Prince and I think the sight of her in a pair of thigh high boots and fishnets will be worth the price of admission alone!

Miss you pumpkin,
Rory and Mr. Paws xxx

20th September

Dearest Rachel,

Almost made a terrible *faux pas* with your mother; so terribly sorry, didn't realize the material was for you, darling. I'm sure the curtains will look lovely when they're up! Think I got away with it, though, as I rapidly changed subject and insisted that she join the costume team. With her sewing skills, we're bound to fit Fat Janet into a fitted waistcoat; might need to add in a few extra fabric panels but I'm sure your mum will be up for that challenge!

I'm not sure if your mum told you but 'Cinderella' has been cast and whilst I'm not convinced we'll be winning any Oscars, I think we'll manage.

Cinderella: Tina (We'll have to work on the voice, terribly common, but she can sing and dance and as long as she doesn't over-pluck her eyebrows, she certainly looks the part)

Fairy Godmother: Felicity (I swear she was born with a plum in her mouth; she's so posh. She's been instructing Cinderella to say something instead of somefink!)

Ugly Sisters: Your friend Rory and Rob, the fireman (Both were extremely funny in the casting and I think the pairing of those two will have the audience roaring)

Prince Charming: Fat Janet (She's just started Weight Watchers, apparently, so I'm going to wait and watch as she becomes a size zero in the next 3 months!)

As for the other parts, we have the usual faces, Phillipa Trott,

Kelly Hotpants, Trevor 'Wooden-acting' Parker, Horace, Jenny. J and Jenny. K and, for her 60th year in the Society, Good Old Iris who has requested to do a tap-dance solo when the pumpkin turns into the coach!

So there you have it. I, naturally, will be directing and - thank goodness - will have Dotty to choreograph the dances and get them all singing!

Think of me honey and pray that Fat Janet doesn't get stuck in the pumpkin coach!

Love,

Miss Elaine xxx

24th September

Dear Rachel,

Big news, darling! You won't believe what I'm about to tell you so I hope you're sitting down. A notice has gone up in Kingsfield saying they are converting it into a Waitrose Supermarket!! The whole village is over the moon. I just had to write to you to let you know. No more budget/basic food for us, my girl, oh no, your father and I will be dining on Waitrose finest! The last time something this big happened to the village was when they built a new Scout Hall but that didn't contain a cheese counter and deli! The only cheese or deli items you could get in Kingsfield were cheesy triangles and a packet of mini savoury eggs!

Naturally, I'll have to buy a proper wicker basket. Can't be seen with a plastic bag in Waitrose, maybe a hessian bag will be acceptable but certainly not the current plastic hold-all!

Love, peace and happiness,

Mum and Dad xxx

P.S: Your father would go and spoil it. Says he'll miss the Kingsfield tinned peaches! Says he's going to go down the road now and stock up before the store closes! Men! Whatever you do, darling, find one who prefers real peaches to the tinned kind!

25th September

Dear Suz,

I think I'm in love! Not only with Barcelona but also with Alberto. I know this might all sound incredibly quick but I need you to experience the magic of La Merce and then you'll understand. However the path of true love never runs smooth so let me rewind and I'll update you on all that happened!

So La Mercè is the Fiesta (it means party, see I'm learning Spanish!) to celebrate the Saint of the city. They used to have this other saint called Saint Eulalia but according to Alberto the people of Barcelona got a bit bored of her so replaced her with Saint Mercè, only Saint Eulalia was sad that the people replaced her so she cries over the celebrations, which normally means it rains, which it did. (Still following?) Anyway, enough of the history lesson and on to the fiesta talk! On my Spanish course I've become friends with a really nice girl from the UK, called Lucy. She's a right giggle, lots of fun and it's certainly nice to have friend to do things with; so the two of us spent the whole weekend exploring the city and trying to do as much as possible. The city is just bustling with things to do, there's live music, stalls

56

selling food, street parties and so much more. I saw this parade with these spooky giant puppets paraded down the street and you know what I'm like with puppets. I almost had a panic attack! Freaky big headed things of old kings and saints and whatever else, fun for the kids but if you have an irrational fear of puppets, it's hell! Poor Lucy had to take me for a jug of sangria just to calm down. Have to say it did help though; after 3 glasses each I found the giants quite funny! (Yes I'm still a lightweight drinker!)

Apart from said puppets we also visited the harbour, which was full of tall ships from around the world. My Dad would have loved it. I took a few photos of the sails and rigging and Lucy made me pose embarrassingly with a Russian sailor holding a rope, going to send them to Dad, as I know he'll like them.

Finally onto Alberto... Well all was going fantastically well until the Correfoc (no I'm not swearing, it means fire-runs in Catalan. I would move to a country where they speak two bloody languages, if one wasn't already enough for me!) Well, there we were enjoying this display of firecrackers and people in costumes when all hell broke loose! I'm telling you, Suz, it was like Bonfire night without any health and safety rules. It just wouldn't happen in Britain, the people couldn't cope. People running down the street, throwing firecrackers and waving flaming sticks in your face while dressed as demons. Bloody mental! As you can imagine her majesty here slightly freaked out and I lost Lucy in all the chaos. (By the way the chaos is all part of the plan, to my eyes it was a crazy mess but actually it's very traditional and people choose to take part!)

So without a mobile phone and no Lucy in sight I decided to head back home and just as I was escaping from the madness of the correfoc I literally bumped right into Alberto, knocking him over and falling on top of him. Then after a few minutes of awkward apologizing, he asked if I wanted to join him to see the final fireworks to end the celebrations. I told him if they were anything like the ones in the correfoc I'd rather 'foc off' home but he reassured me they were worth seeing so I joined him. We then walked across the city to Placa d'Espana facing Montjuic and managed to squeeze through all the people to find a spot right near the Magic Fountain — (you'd love it, it's a huge fountain which changes colour while songs are played. I'm so taking you and

Rory there when you visit.) Then, soon after that the fireworks began and oh what fireworks! Suz, they were magical and what made them more magical was the fact that Alberto reached out and squeezed my hand as the final rockets went off to Freddy Mercury singing 'Barcelona'. The colours, music, atmosphere and company were all perfect until Saint Eulalia got jealous and decided it was time to put out the 'fireworks' and absolutely pour down with rain. So for the second time that night I was engulfed in chaos as people ran for cover – and when I looked up Alberto was gone.

I finally got home, soaked to the skin and the first thing I did was search out my phone. I had a sweet text from Lucy saying she had run screaming from the correfoc but managed to get home just before the rain hit and how she had loved spending the weekend with me. I was hoping to have something similar from Alberto but sadly not. Perhaps tomorrow?! So my love, that's my exciting news. Certainly not had a Guy Fawkes Night as eventful!

Big kisses,

Rach xx

26th September

Dear Mum and Dad,

A new Waitrose, how classy! Next time I'm back home for the weekend I'll expect a high-class meal of roast partridge, dauphinoise potatoes and a side of purple sprouting broccoli, followed by a strawberry parfait with a splash of raspberry coulis!

Glad you're helping out with the panto, Mum, it sounds as if Miss Elaine could do with the support. You'll be pleased to know that I will be back to see it, as I've booked my flights and will be back in the UK for a whole festive week! Make sure you stock up on goodies especially for my arrival! I'm particularly craving sausage rolls and cheese straws!

You'll be pleased to know that my curtains are finally up! God Save The Queen! I hired a local handyman to help me out and he did a super job. Think I'm going to have him come round next week to put up some pictures I bought this week at a local flea market in the city. There are so many creative people here it's always so inspiring. If I find out there's enough time around my new job, which I start next week, I've decided to take up baking again. I was always a great baker and loved creating new recipes but I kind of gave up due to always being so busy at work. Hopefully the job here will be a bit more relaxed like the people and I'll be able to get cooking again on a more regular basis and not just on special occasions!

I must say I'm feeling a little anxious about starting the new job though. I popped in to the Hotel yesterday (looks very posh) to hand in some paperwork and saw this rather mean-looking woman yelling at one of the cleaners. I'm not quite sure who she was, I'm just hoping she wasn't anything to do with my post as receptionist. I worked with one crazy bitch (pardon my language!) but Victoria Plum was a truly terrible woman to work for and I so don't want to repeat that experience. I officially start on Monday and am determined to make a good impression. After all, I was working at the Windmill Hotel for six years and I know the role very well, I just hope my basic Spanish is good enough, though. They did say at the interview they mostly had international guests who spoke English and that my beginners' course would do, so lets hope they're right! I will keep you updated on how it goes Mum. I'm already predicting there will be a few good stories to tell.

Lots of love,

Rachel xxx

P.S: You were right about the winner of Bake Off. I certainly didn't think he'd win but was ever so pleased for him. Loved the wedding cake he designed at the end. Perhaps one day I'll design my own wedding cake! Glad you had fun with Miss Elaine and Mrs. Ashley (Still find it hard to call her Gill after she taught me H.E for so many years!). Send them my love.

30th September

Dear Rach,

Love is in the air! Do, do, do, do, do, do! Love is in the air! Hee, hee! You go girl! It all sounds very promising, I hope he's texted you. He'd be a fool not to! I'm dying to see a picture of him. I've got a picture in my mind and for some reason he's always shirtless with a lovely muscular hairy chest and tan... am I right?

Sadly my love affair with Mr. Stevens was short lived but I'm not too disappointed, as I've finally landed a date with Mr. Body Pump himself! He's taking me to the cinema on Friday night followed by dinner and goodness knows whatever else! I'm practically dribbling at the thought. Needless to say, I told Miss Barbie Sunshine, who actually looks about 50 from close up. She smiled through gritted teeth and said how happy she was for me, then she told me she was bored of Body Pump anyway and was going to take up Body Balance with Dean. So looks like it's "goodbye to Barbie!"

When do you start your new job, honey? Monday? If so, good luck! I'm sure you'll be fabulous. Did you find yourself a lovely new European wardrobe to wear? I'm sure Zara will be able to cater for all your needs. I do miss my shopping partner, though, I stupidly suggested going shopping with Pippa (the barmaid at the New Moon) the other day and ended up spending two hours in Primark. It was like shopping in a jumble sale with a load of wild animals in bumper cars. I've never seen such a mess of a shop - and the people weren't much better, either! My OCD was at factor 10, I'm telling you. Not that I'm trying to replace you, that would be impossible, but I am looking for a new mate to fill the Rachel-shaped hole you've created in my life. Pippa, sadly, isn't the one to fill in, if the three cheap hoodies, the two pairs of flesh-coloured leggings and the gold hooped earrings she bought are anything to go by! Your new friend Lucy sounds much nicer. I hope she's not as nice as me though! Would hate to be downgraded just because we live in different countries.

Anyway, forget my woes and get yourself out in that lovely Spanish sun. Can't believe you're still having beach weekends in September!! Lucky cow!

Love you loads,

Suz x

Chapter 3
October – Getting To Grips

1st October

Dear Rachel,

Pinch, punch, first of the month and no returns! Hello darling, how are you? Good luck for your first week in the new job. Your father and I are both thinking of you and know it will go well. It's funny, actually, because after we were talking about your new role, we started reminiscing about our old jobs. We talked for hours about it so thought we'd share our job highs and lows with you - when I say we'll share, naturally I mean I'll share while your father watches repeats of Poirot. He's watched the same episode twice before and he still doesn't know who the murderer is! Some detective he'd make!

Job highs and lows:
High – My job high was working as a flight attendant for British Airways for 30 glorious years. As you know Mummy was all glamour in those days, jetting off around the world to all sorts of places. These days I can hardly push a trolley round Tesco, let along a jumbo jet! Your father's job highlight was slightly less glamorous but for him it was his high point and that was fixing Pam Saint Clement's fridge-freezer. She's the one who plays Pat Butcher in EastEnders. Well, according to your Father, she's really rather posh and she doesn't actually wear big dangly earrings! Who would have thought it! He also knows for a fact that she's posh because he looked inside her fridge and said it was filled with food from Marks and Spencer! I've been known to buy a few party nibbles from M&S for special occasions but a whole fridge full! He says it was his high point because after he had

fixed her fridge-freezer she made him a turkey sandwich and offered him a glass of champagne. I know it was nearing Christmas but really! Think she was secretly trying to get him into bed myself but she's not his type!

Anyway those were the job highs, now for the lows!

Low – The job lows were pretty low (I'm sure after working with that awful Victoria Plum woman your lows can't get any lower, though, darling). My job low was working behind the counter of a local bakery when I was 18 years old. As you know Mummy was a smart young thing, just trying to save up some money for my career in aviation. Well, the job itself was fine but this one man used to come in every morning and ask how firm my buns were. This went on for 6 months until I couldn't take it any more and hit him over the head with a French baguette. Naturally I was fired but it was so worth it. Who knew I would then go on to marry that man! Hee, hee! Your father's always been a handful!

Meanwhile your father's career low was apparently when he started training as an electrician and the store he worked in only had plain digestives at break time! Hopefully, darling, that's all the worries you'll have to put up with. (By the way, do they have biscuits in Spain?)

Well, enough of the reminiscing; must dash as I'm off round Miss Elaine's house to run through the costume list. At present she wants the main characters to have 5 costume changes each. I think she thinks it's a blooming West End show. They can have two costumes each and I'll accessorize with bows and ribbons to make it look like they've changed costumes. Your friend Rory is a laugh, though, he's drawn some ideas for his ugly sister costume for me. He's going to look like Lady RaRa at a firework party by the time I'm finished with him! See Mummy can be down with the trends, I know all about Lady RaRa. Since popping along to Panto rehearsals I'm becoming well acquainted with all the latest things and modern sayings. The other day one of the young dancers asked me if I could twerk, I told her I'd been twerking all my life. After all, I told her if you don't twerk hard you'll get nowhere in life. (I do take it 'twerk' is a new way of saying work?)

Love, peace and happiness,

Mum and Dad xxx

1st October

Dear Suz,

I think I've made a terrible mistake. The job has turned out to be a nightmare! I literally have the Boss from Hell. Madam Sanchez is a devil woman! She's like an evil Roald Dahl book character in human form and makes Victoria Plum look like Mother Teresa! My first week has been like a form of endurance testing, I'm telling you! I kept looking around to see if there was some kind of film crew about to spring out and say "got you!" but they were never there. Instead I'd just see the ever-frowning face of Madam Sanchez looking at me as if I were some kind of complete moron!

So I started on Monday in my new raspberry Zara top and matching pencil skirt, looking - and feeling - rather swish and professional. Within a minute of getting there, however, my confidence was blown right out of the water when 'The Evil One' pointed out that I wasn't working in a circus and, henceforth, I was only to wear only black. She then ushered me behind the hotel reception desk and told me she would be observing me all morning with the aim of providing feedback after my morning's work. I then asked her where Lola was, the lovely woman who had hired me for the job and she said she had been transferred to a hotel in Madrid and that she had replaced her! (Boo for me!) Anyway, that morning I checked people into their rooms and personally thought I did a great job (I even used some of my basic Spanish when the customers were Spanish) However Madam Sanchez thought otherwise and gave me the following feedback!

1. I was being too friendly. Apparently I asked too many questions and therefore was wasting the customers' time! I had simply said 'How are you, did you have a nice flight?'

2. When I handed the customers the key to their room I was apparently breaking a health and safety rule by putting it into their hand instead of sliding it across the desk. According to Madam Sanchez, by potentially touching the customer's hand I could be contaminating the entire staff at the hotel and risk spreading germs, SARS and I guess even the Plague!

3. As well as wearing the wrong colour, my skirt was also 3 cm too short and had to be below the knee. Ahhhhh! I felt like I was back in Secondary School with that dreadful Mrs. Boomer bellowing at me for looking like a cheap

slut for showing my knees.

What am I going to do? I dare not tell Mum and Dad any of this as they'll worry. I guess I'll just have to face it head on and hope the dragon eases off.

Lots of love,

Rach xxxx

P.S: Don't worry, honey, you're still my best buddy. Having said that, receiving a parcel of British food goodies would cement you in that position! (Hobnobs please!)

P.P.S: Still no reply from Mr. Spain. Oh boo! I was so excited about seeing more of him.

3rd October

Dearest Rachel,

You are a chip off the old block. Your mother is a blast! She's certainly been bringing some much-needed life to the village hall for rehearsals. My chorus this year is as animated as the scenery; in fact I think our wooden backdrop has more life than they do! Hopefully, your mum's costumes will bring some colour to their sourpuss faces. I really don't know why some of them come but they do and year after year Clare Moore acts more and more like a piece of wood!

The principals are working out well, though, and even Fat Janet seems to have lost a little weight. She says she's joined the local gym that your friend Suz goes to. With a little bit of luck she'll shed a few more pounds and the velvet wedding jacket won't need the extra panel sewn into it after all! Rory's doing a fine job and he's sparking off nicely with Rob the Fireman. Rob's got plenty of admirers already; even your mum says she's looking forward to measuring his inside leg measurement!

How are things with you? Job all good? I know they're missing you at your old place. Sandra says the new girl is nice but a bit dim. She somehow managed to book two couples into the same room. Wouldn't have been too bad but when she opened the room the first couple were 'busy' - if you know what I mean - and to make matters worse it was the local conservative councillor and his secretary who were the ones getting 'busy'!

Hope to hear from you soon,

Love,

Miss Elaine xxx

P.S: I know it's way off but when you're back over Christmas, you must come to my Christmas party. It's going to have a Winter Wonderland theme! Was thinking about getting a horse drawn sleigh but don't want my guests stepping over piles of horse poo on the front doorstep!

8th October

Dear Mum and Dad,

Well, I've completed a week in my new job and it's certainly interesting. The people are friendly and the hotel itself is beautiful. My boss is a little on the strict side but I seem to be handling things just fine. All jobs come with their high's and low's, as you know from your previous letter! You do make me laugh, Mum. I love all your funny stories and general ramblings. It's not quite the same as having a gossip over a cup of tea and a blueberry muffin but it is really rather lovely getting letters in the post and reading them whilst relaxing on the sofa. I can picture you and dad so clearly.

What with the new job and all, I've had quite a quiet week really. After five days being back at work and using my brain again I decided to have a chilled weekend and just hung around the flat making it look homely. I've found out there's a super secondhand market on Sundays on the Rambla Raval and you can get all sorts of lovely things. I discovered this one stall, which sold gorgeous prints so bought three to put up in my 'el flato'. They've got red in them so will look fab next to the Union Jack curtains. Think

I may need to get my handyman back round to help me put them up, though.

So there we go, not so much to tell this week but I'm sure there'll be more stories next time.

Lots of love,

Rachel xxx

9th October

Dear Suz, you great big tart!!

Where are you? I've not had one of your disgusting WHSmiths animal-themed cards for at least two weeks and I'm dying to hear how your date with Mr. Body Pump went. I'm guess that's why you've not been in touch. Either it was a great success and he's been giving you one on one sessions or nothing came of it, in which case you've been watching weepy movies and eating tubs of ice-cream. Naturally I'm doing the latter at the moment. Still no word from Alberto so my ice-cream tub count has reached 3 which means I'm officially in a relationship with two other men: Ben and Jerry. (Sob!)

Anyway, I've just written the dullest letter to my Mum saying nothing really happened this week when in fact it has; but it's all been so bloody awful I didn't want to tell her as she'd worry about me. But with you I'm letting it all out...

So week one at the Madam Sanchez Academy of Torture was just about survived with the help of a couple of massive glasses of red wine each night. Really, the woman is the meanest person I've ever met; she told me off for smiling too much, told me off for leaving the pen lid off, told me off for not answering the phone within the allotted 2-second time-limit!!! And after working all week, learning routines, welcoming countless guests, and not making one real mistake, she didn't even say "thank you" on Friday. Instead she simply said 'OK, you can go now'. Moody cow!

Next week I've decided to rebel, though, as there's no chance in hell that I'm going to put up with that for the rest of my time in Barcelona.

As a way of trying to switch off from work, I joined a gym on Saturday but that turned out to be a disaster too! Lucy's a bit like you, a 'sporty spice', so she signed me up to her gym at the end of the street. I'm not that into all the machines, really, but I thought I'd give them a go - and to tell the truth, I was doing fine until I decided to try out the rowing machine. I'd never really used one before because the one in the local sports centre back home was always sweaty and damp from the people who used it before me and so I steered well clear of it. This one looked nice and clean, though, so I clamped my feet in and started to row. Well, after 500 meters of back-and-forth rowing, a couple of incredibly hot guys walked past me. The size of their arms and chests rather dazzled me and so I turned to check out their bottoms (terrible aren't I!) but as I did so, I kind of lost balance and fell off the bloody rowing machine with a loud bang. Naturally, everyone turned around and looked but because my feet were still in the foot holds I wasn't able to get up again!! Mortifying! That's when the two guys who I had been perving at came over to help me. Javi and Toni turned out to be two lovely guys but were more interested in each other than me in my pink lycra, rolling around on the floor like some kind of washed-up jellyfish!

Lucy treated me to a coffee and large slice of chocolate cake afterwards to cheer me up but, really and truly, it has been a totally disastrous week and one in which I intend to not repeat any time soon!

Lots of love,

Rachel aka The Pink Single Jellyfish xxx

16th October

Dear Rach,

I'm so sorry for the delay in writing but you guessed correctly. Mr. Body Pump and I have been totally getting it on. Cinema date was a gentle warm-up for what has turned into what I call a physical relationship! Hee, hee! His body is to die for; if chocolate came in human form that's how delicious he'd be. He's also very cute, though, and funny and, yes, generally I am a smitten kitten.

I cannot believe the luck (or lack of it) you've had lately, though. The job sounds a total nightmare! I'd like to come over and give Madam Sanchez a right piece of my mind. Having said that though, honey, jobs tend to suck wherever you are in the world and at least your life in Spain is fabulous. The last picture you sent me was gorgeous; you looked so tanned I almost mistook you for Donatella Versace! (The colour, that is, not the wrinkles!)

I can't believe Alberto never called you back, though. It really is a mystery. Perhaps he lost his phone? Have you tried texting or calling him? I suggest you get him back for some more DIY and then refuse to let him leave the flat until he takes you out on a date!

Tonight Gav and I are going on a romantic 10 mile run along the South Downs and then afterwards the best bit... the shower!

Kisses and hugs for my girl, chin up and think positive.

Love you loads,

Suz xxx

P.S Hope you like your box of goodies. I felt so guilty for not writing, that I knew exactly what to do to make you forgive me.

22nd October

Dear Suz and Rory,

Thank you so much for the box of goodies. You don't know how good it felt to have a real taste from home: PG Tips Tea Bags, Monster Munch, Cadbury chocolate, Birds Custard Powder and Chocolate Hobnobs!!! You really are angels! I also believe you must have added some good luck in there as well as, fortunately, my luck has changed massively this week.

Firstly I arrived into work to find out Madam Sanchez was on a week-long hotel management conference in Madrid! Result! (She had left me a very detailed list of do's and don'ts for the week but at least that can't shout at me and give me evil stares)

And secondly - and far more importantly - I've got a date with Alberto lined up!!! Yippee! You see, whilst I was unpacking my gorgeous goody box of treats, a bag of Malteasers split open and the entire packet rolled all over the floor. Then, when picking them up and scoffing them down (I swear I blew the dust off first) I noticed one of those small business calling cards on the floor by the front door and when I picked it up, realized it was from Alberto. It said

'Hey Rachel, I really enjoyed the fireworks with you. It was a perfect night until someone in the crowd stole my mobile telephone as we were leaving. I hope to see you soon, Alberto.'

So you were right, Suz, he did lose his phone or rather, it was stolen. The pickpockets here are a sneaky bunch. And because the card was so small and I'm a lazy cow who should clean more often, I never noticed it. I'm guessing he left it there soon after the night of La Mercè so it had been there for 3 whole weeks! However all is good; I phoned him up — he's got a new phone now — and I explained how I had mislaid the card; don't want him thinking I'm an untidy cow, after all, and then he invited me to a Halloween party! I naturally accepted and now desperately need to think of a suitable costume that's spooky yet sexy; but before you two get any ideas I want sophisticated sexy not slutty sexy!

So all in all it's been a fabulous week and I'm glad to have the Barcelona lifestyle back on track. How are my two favourite people doing? How's that dog of yours, Rory? Behaving himself I hope! How's that man of yours, Suz? Behaving himself, I hope!

Lots of love,

Rachel xxx

P.S: I know I usually say I want letters rather than emails but as the party is pretty soon, you can email me any 'suitable' Halloween costume ideas ASAP.

23rd October

Dear Suz and Rory,

Thanks for the pictures of the slutty Halloween costumes; I'm really glad you listened to my request! Some of those outfits were just plain pornographic. I mean, really, the vampire bride might as well have been half naked! You'll be pleased to know that despite your efforts to dress me as a cheap Halloween whore, I've opted for comedy witch instead. I know you'd both say it was a ridiculous idea but I think it's good to show off one's sense of humour. Besides, the stick-on nose is hilarious, I look like my Great Aunt Shirley! (See attached picture!)

Happy Halloween, guys!

Wish me luck!

Love Rachel xxx

25th October

Dear Rachel,

There's no use hiding anything from your mother. I can tell from your tone in your last letter that the job is a disaster and your boss is a nightmare and after cornering Suz in Sticky Buns in the village she told me the truth. Well, my darling, here's some advice from your dear old Mum; after all I've had quite a few crap jobs over the years and a few (excuse my language) shitty bosses too!

1. *Don't let them get to you and always keep your cool. I used to look in the mirror in the morning and pretend to paint my work face on when I worked as a secretary at Barrington and Sons. Why, Mr. Barrington was a right old so and so, forever finding fault in my work but I put on my work face and smiled. I then went home and played darts with his face pinned to the board!*
2. *Make friends with the other employees. You'll all bond over mutual hatred for whoever is making your working lives a misery and will probably have a jolly good time behind the bosses back!*
3. *Put together a get-out plan, something to spur you on, something to get you through the darkest days, something even a bottle of Lambrini won't solve. After all dreams don't work unless you do!*

Now, moving on to other topics, my love. Waitrose update!! The store is complete and the food is divine. It's a bit pricey, mind you, but your father and I think it's worth it. The store makeover, however, isn't as dramatic as the makeover of its staff. You'll never believe it but all the old staff members, 'Kung-Fu Brenda' (the one who practically chucked your food down the counter at you), 'Next customer pleeeeeaaassseee' (the one with that awful common accent) and 'Chatterbox Hannah' (the one that could out-talk your Great Aunt Shelly) have had a makeover too. Gone are the rough and ready cashiers and welcome to Brenda 'May-I-pack-that-for-you?' Cooper, Florence 'who-may-I-help-next?' Thomas and, finally, Lauren 'Polite-smile-no-backchat' Davies. It's as though they've all been replaced by robots! Whatever happens at Waitrose Staff Training centres it certainly works and I may be sending your Father there for a holiday!

So my dear, no more letters that aren't 100% honest. It's bound to be a challenging year for you so take it easy, try your best and don't let that old cow Madam Sanchez get you down.

Love, peace and happiness,

Mum and Dad xxx

Chapter 4
November – Victoria Plum

1st November

Dear Suz and Rory,

Ahhhhh!!! My Halloween night with Alberto started as a real-life nightmare. I can already see the two of you creasing up over this so get it all out of your system before getting in touch, because it really wasn't funny at the time. Maybe when I'm 100 and living with a houseful of cats and content to be a crazy old cat woman I'll have a slight chuckle about it, but at the time, all I wanted to do was curl up into a ball of embarrassment and never leave the house ever again. Ever! However, some nightmares have the ability to turn into dreams too!

So after that ever-so-slightly dramatic opening, here's what happened... I had perfected my witch's make up at home in my 'el flato'; a lovely lurid green complexion, stick-on hooked witch's nose, black frizzy wig and black dress (complete with a slightly slutty neckline!) I then hobbled along to the party, which was at Alberto's flat. When the door was opened I naturally said 'Happy Halloween' in my best witches voice then gazed inside in real horror as I realized no one else in the room was dressed up! I almost died of embarrassment, I can tell you.

Alberto, along with the rest of the people in the flat just glared at me with a 'who-is-this-crazy-woman?' look on their faces and for a split second I was about to turn and run. If my broomstick had actually been real I would have flown off for a quicker exit - but then he smiled his delicious Spanish smile and simply asked me if I had done anything new with my hair since he saw me last. This just cracked us all up and, thankfully, the laughing defused the huge embarrassment that I had brought upon myself. After that he personally introduced me to all his friends and after a few vodka and cokes I started to really enjoy myself. Alberto even found a box of wigs and hats in his spare room left over from carnival for everyone else to put on too, so, fortunately after a while they all looked as crazy as I did.

The night then seemed to whizz by and luckily a few of his friends spoke English, so I wasn't left there smiling and nodding like a children's toy all evening. I must, however, try to learn more Spanish as I am still not understanding much, especially when there's lots of people talking at once, then add in the music, the alcohol (3 Spanish-measure vodkas and a shot of tequila!) and my thick black witch's wig and I was pretty much useless! It also turns out I'm rubbish at reading Spanish too...

So initial embarrassment over and done with and the whole dressing up seemed to be behind me - until someone suggested we head out and have some drinks in one of the local bars. Well the others simply had to take off their silly hats and wigs and they were ready to go. I, on the other hand, was emerald green with a hooked nose glued to my face! I tried to make my excuses and go home but Alberto and the others insisted I came too and suggested I simply wash my face and take the nose off, as my witches dress was a simple black dress and fine for going out in. In principle this was of course a good idea - until I got to the bathroom, washed my face with water and realised the face paint wasn't actually face paint at all but real paint and the glue was, in fact, super glue!!! It turned out that I had been in the art section of the shop where I bought it rather than, as I believed, the fancy-dress section!

After scrubbing my face for what seemed like an hour, eventually Alberto came to check on me and in great embarrassment opened the bathroom door to him to reveal my half-scrubbed, witch-nosed, green face. I thought he was going to shut the door in my face but instead he kissed me! Oh it was magical! His soft full lips touching mine, the warmth of his embrace, the green paint smudging all over his face too! He didn't mind, though, and soon we were both roaring with laughter. He told the others to go on while he stayed behind to help me. He sat me down on the toilet and proceeded to apply some sort of chemical to my face, which luckily removed the glue with ease and even the green paint seemed to come off. Maybe it wasn't the most romantic of settings or the way in which I had pictured it but I wouldn't have changed a thing.

We then joined the others in a crowded little cocktail bar (you would both love it!) and I'm glad to say that under its subtle lighting my slightly green complexion didn't seem to stand out too much. After a few more drinks, Alberto walked me home and kissed me goodnight and again I felt like I was melting in his arms. Not a bad end to such a disastrous start to the evening, I must admit. (Huge smile on face!)

All my love,

Rachel xxx

6th November

Dear Rachel,

Well, last night went with a bang! Your father and I decided to go to London for a mini-break. Daring, I know! You know how we're not really big city people but we fancied seeing The Phantom of the Opera as a birthday treat for your father. He doesn't really like birthday parties so this seemed like a nice treat for the two of us. So off we popped on the train up to London. I have to say I was rather concerned that we'd never find the hotel and that we'd be mugged in a back alley but Dad did us proud and got us to our hotel without too much fuss. I must to say, though, the amount of people there is quite ridiculous. All that pushing and shoving just to get from A to B was worse than a jumble sale at the Village Hall!

You would have loved the hotel, though, darling; the bedroom was beautifully decorated and the view across to the London Eye was quite unexpected. A treat in some respects and a curse in others - but I'll come on to that later!

So after unpacking we went for a wander round (I held my handbag tight and your father had a whistle round his neck in case of an emergency). We saw Trafalgar Square, where a pigeon pooped on a woman next to me, then we went in the National Portrait Gallery and pretended to be all arty-farty; but after half an hour we got a bit bored and headed towards China Town. There we saw a wonderful street performer and your father gave him 10p. Then we bumped into your friend Rory with his little dog. He insisted we join him for a drink in Soho so your father and I ended up in a gay bar full of gays. Oh, we had a wonderful time! Rory ordered us both a lovely fruit juice cocktail with an umbrella in it. Went down a treat, it did. After our third one though, I realized they had alcohol in them and I had to be taken outside for a spot of fresh air! After Rory walked me up and down the street a few times, I came back and Dad was surrounded by a group of large men with beards talking about musicals. Next thing we knew your father had managed to get us upgraded to a private box to see Phantom. One of the men, you see, worked as a stage manager and liked your father so much he thought he deserved a birthday treat! So after a rousing chorus of 'Happy Birthday' from all of Rory's friends we were off to the theatre and seated like the Queen and Philip up in our own private box!

I'm telling you, Rachel, it was like a dream come true. Well, the show was a spectacle indeed and also gave me some super costume ideas for the panto ballroom scene. We then thanked Henry the Stage Manager and headed back to our hotel. Then no sooner had we got into bed, all of a sudden there was a huge explosion outside the window. In our excitement we had forgotten it was Firework Night and there in front of us was the London Eye lit up like that awful house at number 42 on Christmas day with all those common Christmas lights outside! It was a treat indeed until a stray firework whizzed through the window of the bedroom and set the fire alarm off! So out we trotted onto the street outside our hotel, your father in his Marks & Spencer pyjamas and me in my pink nighty, surrounded by all the people who had gathered to watch the fireworks. Rather embarrassing, to tell the truth but after having such a wonderful day we didn't really mind. Your father even took his tartan dressing gown off and wrapped it round me. He can certainly be a romantic old so-and-so when he wants to be.

Love, peace and happiness,

Mum and Dad xxx

7th November

Dear Rachel,

Greetings from Pantoland! Rehearsals are going surprisingly well, apart from the usual things. Maybe the chorus is arguably the most lifeless ever. I'm thinking of replacing them all with wooden puppets as I feel the audience would respond to them better. Fortunately the principals are rather better; having said that, some of them have gone to the other extreme by acting so O.T.T. they could be in the cast of a Spanish Soap Opera! Phillipa Trott, in particular, has embraced the role of the Queen and keeps trying to outshine Cinderella and the Fairy Godmother. We rehearsed the ballroom scene the other day and her entrance was so flamboyant you would have thought Elton John had come on stage!

The costume fittings are going very well though and your mum is doing a super job. So far she's made 6 gingham skirts, 3 milk maid blouses and Cinderella's dress of rags, which apparently used to be your favourite dress before you spilt red wine down it on your 21st birthday. (Was that the same birthday you fell in the village pond?!)

Anyway, enough Panto talk; how's it going with Mr. España? Rory has been telling me all about him. Sounds like a right dreamboat! I once had an affair with a gorgeous Spaniard. Miguel Rodríguez. He was a perfect gentleman and absolutely loaded! Spent a whole summer cruising around the Med. on his yacht. It was only when we got back to port in Barcelona that I realised he wasn't quite the gentleman he painted himself to be. There were 5 police officers waiting for him and a warrant for his arrest for impersonating someone else. Apparently he wasn't really Miguel Rodríguez but, in fact, Bill

Turner from Leeds. He had a Spanish mother so looked the part and the rest was down to his years doing amateur dramatics, apparently! Well, he fooled me so he must have been good. He was sentenced to 8 years in prison for identity theft amongst other things. I was only questioned then released. All very dramatic! As you can imagine, I relished every minute of it!

Anyway darling must head off, as I need to work out how to fly the Fairy Godmother onto stage in Act 2.

Lots of love,

Miss Elaine xx

9th November

Dear Rach,

Rory and I laughed our pants off when we read your last letter. Sometimes I wish you were just on Facebook like the rest of the world but then other times, like on this occasion, I love the way your stories are just for a select few of us. It makes me feel very special and lucky to have such a bonkers friend like you! Green paint!!!! You really do need to improve your Spanish skills; how are the lessons going, by the way? When's your first exam? I hope there's not a section on choosing the right cosmetics!

At least it all ended well, though. Bertie (that's what Rory and I call your Alberto) sounds like a dream! Mind you, I bumped into Marcus Flynn in the village yesterday and he's a total dream too. He asked after you, naturally, and wanted to know if you'd be back for Christmas. I think he's pining for you. Still he had his chance and blew it! Spain 1 - England 0!

Talking of blowing it, I think Gav the Body Pump instructor has. While he's divine to look at he really has the personality of a potato. And not even an exciting potato, like one covered in cheese and bacon or a roast potato, which is crispy and fluffy inside; no, he's just a dull old round potato. While the sex has, admittedly, been amazing, I'm afraid the conversation revolves around sport, diet, football, carbs and sport. Yawn! Plus I introduced him to Rory one night and Rory couldn't keep his eyes off Gavin's chest! He's a right tart that one! No, it's time to move on and find someone a little more intellectual, I feel. It does mean I may have to give up my Body Pump class but it's probably not a bad thing as if I had to do another sit up I'd probably die! I might quit the gym, in fact, and save some money for my return to Oz next month. I've decided to stay for a whole month, as I've not seen the folks for so long. Mum and Dad have apparently invited the whole family for a traditional Ozzie Christmas BBQ on the farm so if that's the case it will take us a month to eat all the food they prepare! Just feel gutted that I wont be in the UK when you're home, though. Still, Rory and I have booked time off work for February and are already coming up with ideas for our Carnival outfits! They won't be requiring green 'face' paint however!

Love you, you silly cow!

Suz xxx

14th November

Dear Mum & Dad,

Lovely talking on the phone the other day; I was so
glad you enjoyed your time in London for Dad's
birthday. When your letter arrived I just had to call
you to hear more of the details. I might even plan in a
little London break next year some time and see a
show myself. Perhaps Dad's friend from the theatre
could get me a couple of good tickets!

Since we chatted last not much has happened really.
Work has been as rubbish as ever. Madam Sanchez
has been her usual scowling self but thankfully I've
become friends with the doorman' Carlos; he's in his
60's and has worked at the hotel for forty years.
He's been very kind to me and as it's a little cold
outside at the moment (Spanish cold, however, is not
British cold - Dad would still be walking around in
shorts) Carlos pops in from time to time and chats
to me in the reception area. He really makes me laugh
with all of his stories and tales about the hotel over
the years. He also hates Madam Sanchez as much as
I do and fears that she'll try to replace him with
someone younger. I think he's too popular with the
regular visitors though, so she can't do anything

99

about it. It must feel terribly sad to get old and feel like you're no longer any use to people.

Having said that my neighbour, Belén, amazes me! She invited me in for a cup of coffee the other day and told me she was 93 years old! Well that's what I think she said; you see, she doesn't speak any English and my Spanish is still very basic. I mostly nod and smile and listen for key words. Mum, you'd just love this woman, though. She lives on the 7th floor like me and climbs the stairs almost every day. I swear her social life is busier than mine. As far as I could translate, she goes to the market every Monday to buy her shopping (the markets here are gorgeous and always have the freshest produce), on Tuesdays she goes to the park to play a game of some sort. I'm guessing chess rather than hide and seek for example! On Wednesdays she stays at home and does her washing. I didn't really catch what she does on Thursdays but I think there was a swimming pool involved. On Fridays she meets up with her friends in the local square and in the evening she either does flamenco dancing or goes to watch it (at 93 I'm guessing it was the latter). Then at the weekends, her family visit her and take her out for the day or she stays at theirs to see the grandchildren. I just hope when I'm her age I'm as active as she is. I think it must be the diet of fresh fruit and veg and the olive oil. Mind you, the Spanish have bread with everything and that's not the healthiest thing in the world. Perhaps matched with an active lifestyle and living on the 7th floor the bread doesn't have the same effect!

Only a little over a month until I see you guys! Can't wait to give you both a big hug. Miss you.

Love,

Rachel xxx

14th November

Dear Miss Elaine,

Love receiving your letters. They put such a big smile on my face! I think I need to pick your brains further on dating tips too, you sound like you're much more experienced than I am! Having said that, things with Alberto are going very nicely indeed. I'm sure Rory has probably told you about the Halloween incident; well, since then we've been out twice more and apart from a few 'mishaps', our dates have been a success. The first date was for a lovely dinner in a restaurant overlooking the city. Barcelona really is gorgeous at night. The skyline is really dramatic and once the Sagrada Familia is complete I'm sure it will be even more special. The dinner was delicious and we had a marvelous time apart from a slight 'flying food' incident! Picture that moment in Pretty Woman where Julia Roberts goes to eat snails and one flies through the air; well, replace that with the head of a prawn which I accidently let fly out of my hand and which landed in front of the woman on the table next to us and you get the picture. She didn't see the funny side but I was pleased to see Alberto did. In fact, he laughed so much he almost choked on his gazpacho!

The second date happily didn't involve flying food but was just as enjoyable. He took me on a guided tour of the city and we wandered round some of the more unusual barrios (neighbourhoods). It was so interesting to see some of the sights that aren't featured in the guidebooks. The Greek Theatre in Montjuic is certainly a hidden treasure and the gardens are just so atmospheric, I can't wait to see them when the roses are out in the spring. Perhaps once panto is out of the way you can plan a mini-break and come and visit, Miss Elaine? My flat is only small but I've bought a blow up bed for the lounge for when visitors come.

I'm enjoying all the pantomime news. Can't wait to see the show. Mum's booked us seats in the front row so we'll be able to clearly see the wood grain of the chorus! LOL! I'll sit next to Dad just in case he falls asleep. I can't believe his snoring disturbed the actors on stage a few years ago when Jemima King put on that awful production of Blythe Spirit. It was some of the worst acting I've ever seen on stage EVER but for dad snoring so loudly made Wendy Tamworth go blank and forget her lines - it was so embarrassing. Dad even tried to blame the Vicar's wife, which made it even worse! Anyway must dash, off to

Spanish class, where tonight we're learning how to describe where we come from. How would you describe good old Latchington?

Lots of love,

Rachel xxx

20th November

Dear Rachel,

Loved hearing about your new friends. Your father said why weren't you mixing with people your own age but don't listen to him. I told him I expect you had plenty of chums to go out with. I told him you'd hardly be off out partying with dear old Belen at the weekends no matter how active she is!

I've been rather busy this week too, darling. We had an 'interesting' flower-arranging expert on Wednesday who specialized in special occasions. She started well with a birthday arrangement using mostly bold flower choices and leafy foliage. It went swiftly downhill, however, when she started adding balloons to the piece. As soon as the first balloon popped I knew we'd have problems and I was right. The sudden noise shocked half of the biddies in the front row and Mrs. Parsons fell off her chair! The arranger, Helen, carried on regardless but after the third balloon popped and Mrs. Vine wet herself, I decided to intervene and I suggested Helen should move on to the next arrangement. Unfortunately, the next special occasion arrangement was 'funerals'. Well, seeing as half the dears are in their 90's the topic was a little close to home and set Mrs. Tinker off right away. Her husband of 70 years had only been buried the week before and Flower Club had been supposed to take her mind off things for a few hours! The last thing she really needed was someone showing her how to make the perfect funeral wreath! So once again I had to stop Helen and swiftly steer her on to her final floral arrangement, which, luckily, had a Christmas theme and the old dears seemed to enjoy that. Who knew flower arranging could cause so much drama?!

Your father's been good this week and has stocked up with logs for the winter months. We do get through a lot of logs in the log burner, you know, so it made me happy to be prepared for the cold days to come. As a reward, I am knitting him a new scarf. Everything these days is homemade, darling, your Mother is back in fashion, you could say. All these overpriced Cath Kidston and Kirsty Allsop creations are just things I grew up making with old scraps of materials and a sewing kit. I can't believe how much people pay for a bit of old-fashioned fabric turned into an apron or purse. I might set up my own business with your Great Aunt. We'd be rolling in it if we charged the same as Cath Kidston does for a tablecloth and napkin set recycled from an old bedspread from the 1950's!

Love, peace and a Cath Kidston handbag,

Mum and Dad xxx

22nd November

Dearest Rachel,

How are things? Good? Bumped into your Mother the other day and forced her to give me your address. Just had to write to you. What's the new job like? Are they as efficient over there? I've heard the Spanish are ever such lazy people. I've not there been myself – too much sun, I'd come out in heat rash and the food would bring on my IBS. Did I ever tell you that I had an irritable bowel?

All simply grand here since you left. New girl is simply wonderful. Very organized and slim too. No trouble squeezing past her at the front desk! Where exactly do you work now? Has it a website? Would be interested in comparing standards between England and Spain. They have a lot of cockroaches don't they?

Your mother looked well. Said she was helping out with the local pantomime, nice of her to help less fortunate people. Won't be going myself, though – once saw a show there – it was awful and a man snored the whole way through the second act.

Packing for a weekend break now with Kevin. He says it's a surprise. That's the wonder of having a mobile home – you can just shoot off whenever you want. Understand you don't use the technology much for communicating, instead you like to receive letters – probably best as you weren't always that good with the online booking system at the hotel. The amount of times I had to correct your mistakes! Ho, ho! Fun times!

Now that I have your address will write again.

Yours truly,

Victoria

22nd November

Dear Rachel,

I'm so sorry I've done something awful! I gave your address to that terrible Victoria Plum woman who you used to work with! Well I didn't actually give it to her; she forced it out of my hands. You see I was just doing a spot of shopping in the village and popped into the fabric shop to pick up some bits and bobs for the panto. Miss Elaine wanted more bows on Cinderella's Ball Gown - honestly by the time all these bows are on it she's going to look like one of those crocheted dollies that your Grandad stuck over the toilet roll to hide it! Anyway, I was just about to post your last letter when she spotted me and ran over. I had one hundred and one questions fired at me and then she spotted the letter in my hand and saw it was addressed to you. Next thing I knew she had pulled out a notepad and pen from her massive handbag and jotted it down. I'm afraid I couldn't do anything about it but I did lie and say you hardly wrote back and said that the post wasn't very reliable, so if you didn't write back she shouldn't take it personally! My goodness, though, what a creature she is! How did you put up with her for so long? No wonder you resorted to leaving the country after working with her every day for 6 years. I'm surprised you didn't move even further away!

Anyway perhaps she won't write; she's not the most interesting person in the world, is she? She mostly spoke to me about her work, the new girl and her camper van. All very dull.

Love, peace and happiness,

Mum and Dad xxx

P.S: Is there anything specific you want for Christmas this year? I'm going to start my shopping at the weekend and want a few ideas to get me going. Your father said he wanted a night out with Sandra Bullock so I bought him Gravity on DVD! That will show him!

24th November

Dear Suz,

Sorry for delay in writing but I've had a busy couple of weeks. I have to say I was tempted to sign up to Facebook but I know if I did my year of letter writing would be over and I really want to see it through. Besides, I know if I did join Facebook I'd end up sitting at home all day wasting my time checking up on people and waiting for someone to message me. It makes me feel so much better writing my letters and coming home at the end of the day and finding out I have letters to read. The postman must be constantly in and out of my building; lucky for him my post box is on the ground floor and not on the 7th! Curious thing is I've never seen him. Wonder if he's a hottie? I imagine with all the walking about he does he must have amazing muscular tanned legs!

Must stop fantasising about imaginary postman, though, as after all, I have my own Spanish hottie! Dating is continuing very nicely indeed and you might say I am officially smitten. Oh Suz, when I look into his gorgeous brown eyes I just want to rip all his clothes off there and then. However I am determined to be a lady and not sleep with him too

111

soon - is next weekend too soon? Hee hee! Next week is the beginning of December and the official turning on of the Christmas lights in the city. I thought it could also be the perfect time for him to turn me on too!

Sorry to hear about Gavin being a potato; however, I've always said there are plenty more potatoes in the field! Or something like that! Maybe when you're back in Oz you'll have someone waiting for you like I have back in the UK! I really don't believe Marcus Flynn is pining for me, though, and even if he were there's nothing to be done about it. I have a new life and a new man in Spain and he just isn't part of it. I am now a patatas bravas girl and a plain old roast potato isn't enough to satisfy me!

Chat soon, honey; I'll give you a Skype over the weekend and you can help me pick out the best bra and panties combo all set for the BIG turning on session!

Love you,

Rach xxx

28ᵗʰ November

Dear Rach,

Mr. Paws and I are missing you. Well strictly speaking, he's never met you but I miss you and he wants to meet you. What date do you arrive back again and do you need a place to stay or are you at your Mum and Dad's? If so I suggest a two centre holiday with them and with me, so choose your dates and let me know so I can inform Daniel Craig he can't come this year.

Ok, so panto update: I know Miss Elaine writes to you but she's the director and is biased so here's the honest truth... it's complete shit! Well not completely shit but pretty shit. I'm good, naturally, and my other ugly (not so ugly in real life) sister, Rob, the sexy fireman, is also very good. The leads, though, are like extras in a bad Joan Collins TV movie. Cinderella can barely remember which character she's playing and Fat Janet, as the Prince, thinks she's on an episode of Hi-de-Hi! Mind you, she has lost a lot of weight and, fair dos to her, might even fit into your old principal boy's outfit without an extra panel being sewn into the back of it! The downside, however, is that she's no longer happy Fat Janet but now Angry, Snappy Slimming Janet. The other day I teased her about how when she used to slap her thigh it kept wobbling for the rest of the performance and she almost pushed me off the stage! Think I preferred her when she was fat and happy!

Anyway, I'm glad you're coming to see it. You're bound to

have a real laugh, just try to laugh in the right places, otherwise Miss Elaine won't let you come to her Christmas Party. This year she's pulling out all the stops and says she's going to hire a snow machine to give it a Winter Wonderland theme!

Can't wait to hear more about Bertie. He sounds delicious! I'm currently seeing a guy called Roger. He's a good kisser, great in bed, has a professional job, likes to travel but hates dogs. Shame, really, but Mr. Paws comes first so its farewell to Roger. By the way does Bertie like dogs or is he more of a pussy fan?

Big hugs and dog licks,

Rory and Mr. Paws xxx

30th November

Dear Mum and Dad,

No worries about Victoria Plum. I can just imagine
her blocking your way to the post-box as she prised
the envelope out of your hand. She always pushed me
out of the way when the top tipping customers
arrived so she'd get the money and I'd be stuck with
the fussy regulars who always complained that their
showers were too hot or cold and would leave you
50 pence if you were lucky. I've not written back to
her yet and not sure I will. I have a feeling her letter
may have 'disappeared' in the post and not made it to
me. Hee, hee!

I'm glad I don't have to put up with her any more
but I'm not exactly in job heaven either, though, with
Madam Sanchez being her delightful self. The hotel is
having a quiet spell at the moment, until it gets busy
again in the lead up to Christmas, which means I have
to put up with her breathing down my neck even more
than usual; and poor Carlos has to stand out in the
cold for longer periods until she disappears into her
office to sort out her paperwork. When she does so,
I run to the window and tap on it three times. He
then pops in for a quick chat until a customer

115

arrives or the Spanish Dragon rears her head again. In the new year I think I'll start looking for another job, something that makes me feel I'm using my creative talents and something I enjoy. In the meantime, however, I'm going to keep my head low and get on with it. Only two and a half more weeks, then I'll be flying home for Christmas!

Love,

Rachel xxx

P.S: As for Christmas presents, Mum, I'm not really fussy, as long as they're not too big so that I can fit them into my case. Think small or flat things for example, jewellery!

Chapter 5
December - Home For The Holidays

1st December

Dearest Rachel,

I wrote to you over a week and a half ago so either you didn't get my letter or have yet to find time to respond. Please let me know if your mother gave me the correct address, I'm assuming she wouldn't have given me anything but your real address but I know how forgetful the older generation can be.

We had Mr & Mrs. Walker in the hotel the other day and they asked after you. At first they thought Jenny, your replacement, was you but then I pointed out that Jenny was much thinner and they realised their mistake. They said they were visiting Barcelona in the spring and wanted to know which hotel you were working at. Let me know and I'll pass on the information to them. I'm sure they may even give you a euro tip if you put them into a good room.

Kind regards,

Victoria

7th December

Dear Victoria,

So sorry for the delay in writing to you, but life is so full and fulfilling here, that my free time for correspondence is somewhat limited at times. My new job working at the Hotel (5 star) takes up much of my time, as does my social life with my Spanish boyfriend, Alberto.

Mum wrote to me saying she had seen you and that you were looking a little tired from working so hard. I hope the new girl is fitting in well. I guess she's hit the ground running, taking over all the tricky customers from me. The Walkers were always rather rude, I felt; I wonder why they requested the hotel I'm working at now? Perhaps you'd pass on to them that it's very exclusive and that I'm not sure they'd be able to afford it but I could always suggest some 3 star accommodation similar to the hotels they are used to staying in.

Glad you're managing to enjoy weekends away in the campervan. It must be so liberating to park up somewhere on the side of a motorway and feel like you're away from everything. I'm off up the Costa

Brava this weekend. The beaches are just divine. I'm a
very lucky girl and get hotel discounts through work,
so get to stay in all the best places!

Lovely to hear from you and kind regards,

Rachel

7th December

Dear Rory & Suz,
Sorry for the joint letter but I felt you both needed to hear this news at the same time, hence the shared card (I'm also a fat lazy cow and couldn't be bothered writing the same news twice and stamps are also really pricey here!)

Well here's the news... I can officially announce that over the weekend Barcelona was lit up, not only with the Christmas Lights but also the massive smile on my face after what can only be described as a heavenly night with Alberto. The evening started in the centre of the city in Plaça de Catalunya where he greeted me with a single red rose and a kiss on the lips. We then walked up the main 'posh' shopping street, Passeig de Gràcia (certainly puts Worthing High Street to shame, that's for sure!), which was celebrating the turning on of the Christmas lights by having a late night shopping experience. It was all simply gorgeous, glittering lights, classy shoppers, music playing and my favourite; freebies! Alberto and I couldn't actually afford anything from any of the shops having their 'late night shopping experience' but what we could do was take advantage of their free

121

handouts. We managed to get 3 glasses of cava each, a few posh chocs, a miniature bottle of perfume (one spray and it's gone type of thing) and the pièce de résistance, a mini magnum ice-cream! Alberto had never actually done the whole freebie hunting before but I told him that my Mum was an expert after years of attending jumble sales, car-boots and charity shops and that I'd pass on some top tips to him that I had learnt myself. Well, guys, he was a natural. We treated it like a game and by the end of the evening he was as good as getting a freebie as the best of them. Now I know you're probably rolling your eyes and thinking 'cheapskates' but I have to say the way he played along and made me laugh was much better than any expensive gift from one of those posh shops.

We then grabbed some amazing tapas from a restaurant Alberto recommended (it's so worth dating a local boy!) and then headed home. He walked me to my door as he always does but this time I invited him up my 7 flights of stairs and all the way to heaven! Hee, hee!

Once we were in the flat I made us both a cup of

coffee and we sat on the sofa talking all about our friends and families, about what we want from life and what our favourite colours were. We then started kissing and then didn't stop. He picked me up in his arms and took me to the bedroom and we undressed each other. I was so thankful you helped me pick out the right sexy lingerie; the thought of revealing my usual knickers would have been awful. His pants had obviously been well selected for the night too, a sexy pair of white hipsters that made his skin look like honey, and the best part was what was underneath them. I think you would have both been very impressed! We then spent the whole night having the most amazing sex. I have to say I was thankful that my elderly neighbour was rather deaf, otherwise I think we may have woken her up. Either that or she possible thought I was extremely religious to be shouting "Oh God!" all night long!

Then afterwards he put his gorgeously bronzed Spanishy arms around me and we fell asleep for the last few hours of the night. Then when I woke up he kissed me and we cuddled and talked and I just felt so comfortable. He then jumped out of bed and made me the most wonderful omelette I've ever tasted. Then finally, after a lazy morning in bed, laughing, chatting and having more sex, he showered and left, leaving me in a blissful state of delight.

I'm already craving my next date with him. He said he's going to take me to a concert and introduce me to another of his favourite restaurants. He's learnt quickly how much I love my food and thankfully he's the same. I'm just envious that he eats what he likes and still has an amazing body while I have to maintain my embarrassing gym sessions just to keep the muffin top and bingo wings in check!

Anyway, time to go, guys, how I miss you both. Thanks so much for writing to me. I know it would be simpler with Facebook or an email but there's something so special about writing these letters and I just know one day I'll look back at all the letters you've written to me and smile, something that an email will never really achieve in the same way.

Lots of love,

Rach xxx

P.S: I almost forgot! Do you remember that vile woman who I worked with at the Windmill Hotel?

Her name was Victoria: Mum and I called her Victoria Plum but you always referred to her as Vicky Big Bum because of the way her arse stuck out when she talked to you. Well, she managed to get my address off Mum and send me a couple of right nosey letters that pissed me off. The first I ignored but then she had the cheek to write about a week later again poking her nose into my business. Well in response I sent her a real smug, condescending letter in return and at the time it felt wonderful. But now I have to admit I feel rather guilty because I'm not at all smug or condescending and feel like I've sunk to her terrible level. And it's Christmas soon and she already suffers from having a massive bottom and that must surely having something to do with her being such a nasty cow. Oh well, it's in the post now and it did feel good when I wrote it... Maybe it will stop her getting in touch again and that would be something at least.

8th December

Dear Rach,

How are you? I'm so sorry I've taken so long to write but this year I have been given the class from hell! Oh, the joys of being a Primary School Teacher, thank God the holidays are nearly here before I either crack up or become an alcoholic! I had heard the stories about this class but when Jan told me I was going to move to Year 3 and have them, I tried to block them out and focus on the positive. Well I'm afraid to say the brats and their awful parents have sucked out my positivity and shoved it where the sun doesn't shine. There's one boy in the class who takes the greatest pleasure in pissing me off then smiling at me when I tell him off. I'm not supposed to use their actual names because of confidentiality and all that crap, so lets just call him Demon Child. The other day he even got a pair of scissors and cut a pigtail off one of the girls in the class. How he managed it with a pair of safety scissors is beyond me but, naturally, it was my fault and I got bollocked by both sets of parents and the Head Teacher. I can tell you that night I downed a bottle of red before I even sat down to do my marking.

We've got the Christmas Nativity coming up soon and Demon Child is an angel, of all things. I'm tempted to swap his halo for some horns and a tail before he goes on stage. I just know he's going to spoil it all. Thankfully my teaching assistant, Mrs. Benny is amazing and, being built like a tank, is more than capable of taking on Demon Child or his god-awful mother. Is it me or are kids getting more doolally? I know we had a few buggers in our class when we were growing up but every other one seems to have some mega-issues these days - either that, or their parents do!

I used to love teaching, Rach, but these days it just seems to suck the life out of me. All I do is work or worry about work, I have no boyfriend, I don't see my friends as much as I'd like to and when I do get my holidays I'm so bloody tired I usually slob out and want to be on my own or am ill! I really feel it's time for a change but I'm really not sure what else I could do.

Anyway, enough of my moanings and groanings, how are you, my lovely? How's the job going? How's the Spanish? Must catch up next year some time. I hear you're coming back for Christmas but I'm off to Wales to see my Mum and Dad, otherwise I would have loved to have seen you.

Much love,

Gemma x

9th December

Dear Rachel,

Congratulations on passing your first Spanish Exam! What an achievement! Sorry we weren't in when you phoned but it was nice to come home to such good news on the answer phone. You have done well, 79% is a wonderful start and I'm sure now you know the basics it can only get easier. Your father says he's going to take up a language now, I've suggested English because he obviously doesn't understand me when I ask him to get off his arse and clean out the garage!

Things are all getting festive here at the Cottage. I've sent your father up the ladder today to fetch the Christmas decorations down and then later I'll send him back up the ladders to put up the outside lights (the usual classy white not like number 42's house of horror!) I have to say it's not quite the same without you decorating the house with me but knowing that you'll be back with us very soon, celebrating Christmas, makes me feel very happy indeed. I also have some of the ladies from flower club coming round for a mince pie next Sunday so need to make sure the house looks at its festive best as I know they'll be judging me! Terrible really, it started off as just a cup of coffee and a bloody mince pie yet it's now developed into a yearly 'festive' custom. I'll never forget the year when your father got the hose out to wash the cars half an hour before they came round (quite unknown to me as you can imagine!) and as it was such a cold December the water had frozen by the time they arrived so when I went down to greet them, I slipped arse over tit and had my knickers on show to them all. They then in turn got out the car and did the same as me! Oh, it was a cock up! That was the Christmas I refused to make your father's favourite Christmas pudding. He had to settle for a Kingsfield Basic one instead.

This year there will be no settling for second best, though, my love. No, your dear old Mum has pulled out all the stops and it's going to be a simply wonderful Christmas. I suggest you perhaps eat only celery in the week leading up to your visit otherwise you'll have to pay excess baggage when you leave!

Love, peace and happiness,

Mum and Dad xxx

P.S A warning to you! Apparently, Great Aunt Shelly has been knitting since July and we're all getting something!

11th December

Dear Rach,

OMG!!! Life has been so hectic, honey, and tomorrow I fly to Oz for Christmas and instead of packing, which I should have done earlier this week, I'm writing to you because I've been such a bad friend and haven't sent you one of my vile animal cards lately! So please forgive my handwriting and the lack of the usual niceties but here we go.

1. Have been a very naughty girl and have kind of been shagging both Mr. Body Pump and Mr. Body Balance from my gym. Not at the same time, I hasten to add - I'm not quite that naughty!

2. Long story! Instead of dumping Gavin Body Pump and quitting the gym, as I intended, I ended up joining the Body Balance Class, and having sex with the instructor, Dean, in the room where they keep the yoga mats!

3. Managed to keep this up for 2 exhausting (but incredibly satisfying!) weeks until Gavin and Dean found out about the other then had a massive fight in the gym. However, it wasn't as manly as it sounded and despite their muscular physiques both fought like little girls. In the end, Gavin got pushed onto a moving treadmill that sent him crashing into the set of weights which then landed on Dean's foot.

4. So now both are off work, one with a broken arm, the

other with a broken foot and I've been banned from the gym for life (Humiliating!) On the upside, however, my abs and my bum have never looked so good. I'm not sure whether it was the Body Pump Class, the Body Balance Class, the sex or a combination of all three but I am looking good and ready to hit Bondi Beach as soon as I land in Oz, honey!

I am still gutted I'm going to miss seeing you, though, but am so happy that you're happy and that things seem to be going swimmingly with Bertie. I can't wait to meet him in February when we come over. Anyway, my lovely, have a fab Xmas with your folks, enjoy the panto and Miss Elaine's party and give me a buzz Christmas day!

Love you darl!

Suz xxx

P.S I think I'm going to bring out my own Keep Fit programme passing on a few of my top tips! Might be X rated though so don't share it with your Mum!

P.P.S I'll text you my address, honey, so you can keep your letter writing up.

12th December - Email

Dear Rachel,

I just knew it was too good to be true. Everything had come together for the panto and all seemed to finally be in place when both bloody Tina (Cinderella) and Felicity (The Fairy Godmother) have come down with the flu! It's a disaster! They are both on a mixture of Lemsips, Cough & Cold and honey & lemon but if that fails I've come up with a plan. It's not ideal but your mother and Rory came up with the idea and after they had wafted smelling salts under my nose and had given me a shot or two of brandy to get over the shock of losing not one but two cast members, I was shifted into action.

Find attached a copy of the script. I'm sure Tina will be as right as rain by next week but if she's not, please can you just cast your eye over the script (Cinderella's words are all highlighted in pink, darling)? You once stepped in for Juliet in Roger McTuff's version of Romeo & Juliet at the last minute and did a wonderful job and this time it's only panto, not half as complex as Shakespeare. I will endeavour to learn Felicity's Fairy Godmother part and hopefully all will not be lost.

Please say you'll do it, Rachel, and I will forever be in your debt. And as I will be a Fairy Godmother, will naturally grant your every wish and look out for you for the rest of your days!

A wave of the wand of good health!

Miss Elaine xxx

P.S: Please email me back ASAP darling otherwise I'll have to ask Joan to come out of retirement to play Cinderella and she's just turned 89!

12th December – email

Dearest Miss Elaine,

I am sending positive vibes to both Tina and Felicity but just in case the Lemsips don't work I will cast an eye over the script and do what I can to help you out. However, if I do end up on stage this time next week I will be calling in my Fairy Godmother favours!

Love,

Rachel xxx

P.S: Keep me updated on the flu patients. Here's my Spanish number +34688755731

13th December

Dear Suz,

Well I haven't even arrived in the UK yet and you've probably not even landed in Sydney but I thought I'd send this off so it arrives in time for Christmas. Happy Christmas Suz! Thanks for being such a good friend and for making me roar with laughter every time we catch up and when you write to me.

By the time you read this I will have possibly donned a ball gown and glass slipper as Miss Elaine has just asked me to act as stand-in for Tina (Cinderella) as currently she's in bed with the flu. I'm just hoping she recovers in time, as I wasn't really planning on going to the ball a few hours after landing in the UK. Instead I was hoping to chill out on the sofa watching Christmas TV with Dad whilst eating 'festive snacks' and drinking copious amounts of mulled wine! Oh well, will update you soon enough, I guess!

As for your recent update... No comment. (Tart!) You are shocking Suz but I so like the sound of your fitness regime. I think I'd take out the Body Pump part and the Body Balance bit and just stick to the sex part! Hee, hee! Not sure my waist would end up as thin as yours, though, because after sex I always feel hungry and end up raiding the fridge like a right old greedy guts. Alberto doesn't seem to mind my slight muffin top and love handles, though, so I guess I don't have too much to worry about. I have to say I'm going to miss him while I'm in the UK. I'm starting to really fall for him and think he cares for me too. Well, I guess absence makes the heart grown fonder so perhaps a few weeks between seeing each other will be good. He's spending Christmas with his Mum (his Dad died when he was a child) but he says they'll save the big celebrations for Día de los Reyes (Three Kings Day) on the 6th January. Here in Spain most families celebrate the Epiphany, day the Kings arrived at the manger, by having a big lunch and opening presents. Sounds like an excuse just to have two days for getting gifts, if you ask me!

Talking of gifts, I have currently bought zero Christmas presents and now I'm having a bit of a meltdown as this week I need to buy small or flat gifts for family and friends so they fit in my suitcase, learn a whole pantomime script, just in case the lead is ill and also work at the hotel in possibly the busiest week of the year with possibly the craziest bitch boss ever! Smiling, smiling, keep on smiling!

Will think of you on Christmas Day, honey. Don't burn your baps on the BBQ!

Lots of love,

Rach xxx

P.S Look in the bottom of your case for an Xmas gift from me. Don't ask how I managed to get it there but lets just say I have gays in important places!

22nd December

Dear Suz,

Even though you are probably this minute on the beach tucking into your Christmas Day BBQ, wearing nothing but a skimpy swimsuit, after what I'm about to tell you you'll be wishing you were in freezing old England again.

So I landed in the UK 4 days ago and no longer than an hour after arriving back home to Rainbow Cottage I got a call from Miss Elaine explaining to me that the flu patients hadn't recovered and that I was needed for an emergency dress rehearsal down at the village hall. I barely had time to compliment Mum on the Christmas decorations or wake Dad from his early evening nap but they understood and anyway, Mum said she needed to help alter my costume anyway so together we walked down to the village hall.

I have to say after almost half a year away from everyone it was wonderful to see so many familiar smiling faces and Mum was just glowing with happiness having me home. Miss Elaine gave me a massive hug then swiftly ushered me onto stage where we ran through the entire show. At first it

138

was rather painful, especially as I was probably better than half the people on stage that had been rehearsing for the last 4 months! I was, however, not at all prepared for any of the dance numbers and whilst my acting skills are not too bad - even if I do say so myself - my two left feet (passed on by my Father) made a meal out of the musical/dance numbers. Still Miss Elaine was patient and simply begged me to spend the following morning with Tap Dance Tammy perfecting the dances as best I could. I was also to spend the afternoon practicing the 3 songs I had to sing with Mr. P's the organ player (I tell you Suz, you would have been impressed by the size of his organ!)

So after an epic 5-hour rehearsal I finally got to bed at 1am only to be woken up by the alarm at 7am for Day 2 of what can only be called Panto Boot Camp! It wasn't exactly the start to the Christmas holidays I had planned but it was entertaining all the same and certainly more active than sitting on the sofa watching Christmas movies, eating my own bodyweight in Pringles, Twiglets and After Eight Mint Chocolates.

Learning the dance routines almost killed me,

especially as Tap Dance Tammy started by launching into a routine of taps, kicks, jumps and spins that made River Dance look a breeze. She soon realised, however, that I was not a natural dancer and decided to teach me a simple sidestep tap followed by the classic panto manoeuvre, the grapevine! She seemed disappointed that her wonderful choreography wasn't going to be displayed on stage, yet thanked me for stepping in at such short notice and said that we all had our own gifts and, sadly, dancing was not one of mine. I did feel like telling her that tact wasn't exactly a gift she had been born with but let it go. After all Mr. P walked in with his massive organ (Hee, hee! Makes me laugh every time!), and I was then subjected to 3 hours of X-Factor style vocal training as I practiced the 3 songs I had to sing. According to Mr. P, I hadn't Tina's vocal range but he said at least I sang anything instead of anythink. Apparently, Tina's Cinderella was a little on the common side. Even Mum said she was tempted to make her a Burberry Ball gown with Nike Trainers!

So, my lovely, after day 2 of Panto Boot Camp we were ready to roll - well, as ready as we would ever be. Poor Miss Elaine was slightly manic, what with directing the show and now taking part in it and it didn't help that she hadn't mastered her big entrance by wire that was to be one of the highlights of Act 2. Meanwhile, I also had a last minute panic; Mum had been so busy adapting my ball gown so it would fit that she completely forgot about my dress of rags for Act 1. With less than half an hour to go and certainly no time to change it, I was squeezed into my dress of rags by 3 people and when I looked in the mirror I, how do I put it... I had quite a voluptuous cleavage on display. They all reassured me however that it certainly was a cleavage to be proud of and that Cinderella would have certainly sported the 'heaving-bosomed-milkmaid style'. I wasn't entirely convinced - but have to admit my boobs had never looked so good!

It was then curtain up and tits out! Yes, no sooner than the cast had completed the opening song the curtain lifted to reveal me scrubbing the floor, as Cinderella would do, apart from the fact her breasts didn't pop out of her rag dress due to the scrubbing motion like mine did! Yes, Suz, it was the first time back in the UK for 6 months, I hadn't even said my first line and the first thing that happened were my breasts popping out on show to the entire village, including none other than Marcus Flynn sitting in the front row next to the Vicar!

Thankfully the guy in the lighting booth preserved a bit of my dignity by downing the lights for a moment whilst I hoisted my boobs back into the tiny bit of fabric that made up the rag dress. Being the true professional I am, however, I carried on regardless, though blushing the deepest crimson red, I'm sure - but I have to say it's the first time in years that I've been on stage and had the entire audience's attention (especially the men!). There wasn't the usually muttering, sweet paper unwrapping and secret texting that usually accompanies amateur theatre, oh no, they were all too fixated on my boobs, waiting for them to escape again! For your information, they tried it a further two times in Act 1 - but fortunately I was able to duck behind a piece of set the first time and grab one of the Ugly Sister's fans the second time!

When the interval finally came, Miss Elaine rushed up to me and I half expected her to reprimand me for ruining the show when in fact she gave me a huge hug and told me it was the best audience they had ever had and that once this got round the village the following two shows would be a complete sell out!

She then flew off into the wings – something she didn't do so well on stage in her big entrance; in fact, she did fly on but failed to land and then flew right off again. She did the same thing a further 3 times until she finally gave up and just walked in from the side, which got a huge round of applause. Isn't it funny how people often prefer it when things go wrong? From the look on his face, Marcus Flynn certainly did when he saw my boobs highlighted by two bloody great spotlights – and I suspect the vicar did, too.

Act 2 went a lot more smoothly than the first Act and Rory and Rob the Fireman were fantastic as the Ugly Sisters. I stood watching from the wings when I wasn't on stage and found it very amusing to see Rory getting close to his stage sister. You should have seen him, Suz – every opportunity he could get he was all over him. I'm sure by the end of the show the audience would have left thinking the Ugly Sisters were actually lesbians. Rob, however much he enjoyed teasing Rory and let him feel up his biceps, certainly wasn't gay and at the end of the night I saw him whizz off with none other than Fat Janet – who definitely needs a new nickname as she is looking amazing. There was certainly no bingo wings on display and when she slapped her thigh there wasn't a patch of cellulite to be seen. Good on her, I thought! Obviously Rob was impressed too, much to Rory's disappointment.

Once the panto was finished and the standing ovation finally died down I headed back to change — only to find that Marcus had sneaked backstage and whisked me into one of the dressing rooms where he embraced me and told me how much he had missed me. He complemented me on my obvious acting talents as he looked at my chest and told me to meet him for a drink after the show. He then leaned in as though to kiss me when suddenly Mum appeared and insisted I change out of my ball gown so that they could take it back in to make my boobs stood out more! Not missing a beat, Marcus complemented my Mother on how young she was looking and could see where I got my gifts from, to which she blushed and he scampered off like a naughty boy. Oh Suz!! I'm ashamed to say it was all so sexy, not the part with my mother, but the way he looked at me and touched me and I even though I think I'm falling in love with Alberto, it suddenly made me feel all confused. I don't know what I would have done if he had kissed me. When I eventually got changed and went down the pub, so many people wanted to catch up with me and congratulate me that I didn't get to see him again. Just as well, I guess.

Miss you, honey, wish you were here to advise me but glad you're at home with your folks. Will write again before New Year.

Love,

Rach xxx

P.S Another 2 shows to go and then I can really enjoy my Christmas holidays! I've not even had 5 minutes to tuck into one of Mum's famous mince pies!

27th December

Dear Suz,

Well honey I'm not sure where to start with all the news from the last few days. To say it's been eventful would be an understatement to say the least. Why do things never go according to plan?!

22nd & 23rd December: The last two nights of the panto were a great success and after the news got round that Cinderella's breasts might fall out at any minute the audience was packed (mostly old men from the local pub and half of the village rugby team!) Luckily for me, however, my boobs did not make a reappearance, even though the plunging neckline on my dress still gave all the men in the audience plenty to gawp at, no doubt. Still, I was glad the show was a success for Miss Elaine and I was over the moon to see her receive a big bunch of flowers and even a standing ovation (well from the ones who could stand — the audience did have an average age of about 80 but I'm sure they would have stood if they had been able to!)

24th December: Christmas Eve is possibly my favourite day of the year. I just love being at home, listening to

Christmas music, nibbling on cheese straws and eating far too many chocs and generally hanging out with Mum and Dad. And this year didn't disappoint; Mum and I spent time wrapping up the last presents (I have to wrap Mum's from Dad and she has to do mine as Dad is rubbish at present wrapping), and Dad and I sat on the couch and watched "The Snowman" together. Then in the afternoon I helped Mum prep the veg and turkey, ready for the madness of Christmas Day, when Great Aunt Shelly would be arriving with all her side of the family.

25th December: We now move onto Christmas Day where we did the following things in no particular order: eat, drink Buck's Fizz, go to church, eat turkey and compliment the chef, play party games, argue over who has won the party games, drink a little more, watch the Queen's speech (whilst Mum and Great Aunt Shelly comment on how lovely the Queen's curtain's are!), pull crackers, read naff jokes, unwrap presents, put on fake smiles when presented with one of Great Aunt Shelly's home knitted bobble hats, eat some more, fart after too many spouts, watch Christmas EastEnders, watch Christmas Dr. Who, drink a glass or two of sherry, open the massive tin of Quality Street, fight over the Caramel Kegs, burp, snooze and wake yourself up from farting (if you're Dad or Uncle Jim), wash up, eat Christmas pudding, almost burn down the house when Dad puts too much brandy on the Christmas pudding, scoff down the cheese selection (my favourite bit!) and then finally fall asleep whilst Indiana Jones comes on TV. Perfection in one day!

26th December: After an extremely lazy day stuffing my face with turkey dinner leftovers and watching Christmas movies I attempted to squeeze myself into my party dress for Miss Elaine's Boxing Day Party. After consuming a month's worth of calories in the past three days, however, the zip barely did up and Mum had to practically lever me into it, as if I was one of the Ugly Sisters about to go to the ball! It did, however, finally do up and I headed off to Miss Elaine's looking, despite the effort to get into the dress, rather good, if I do say so myself.

You would have loved it, Suz; Miss Elaine had certainly gone to town. She had hired a snow machine and her entire house and garden was covered in fake snow. It looked like a picture postcard and she appeared from the house looking like a minxy Queen of Narnia, draped in white furs (fake) and a gorgeous satin dress. The inside of the house was divine too. Although not as homely as Mum's house, which smelled of gingerbread and cinnamon, Miss Elaine had decorated inside so that everything looked white and frozen and glistening and magical. That's when I saw Marcus, standing next to the punchbowl, dressed in an extremely dashing tuxedo, ladling out some of Miss Elaine's famous Xmas Punch. He came over and handed me a glass and, naturally, I took a sip and almost spat it all out, as it was about 80% pure alcohol! We then laughed and spent the rest of the night chatting and flirting until he pulled me away into the garden. Oh Suz, I don't know if it was the alcohol or the attention or the feeling that this should have happened before I moved to Spain but it was all so exciting. He then told me that he wished he had made a move before I had moved to Barcelona and that he missed me. He asked me if I were staying permanently or whether I'd be moving back – to which I didn't reply because I didn't really know what to say. I wanted to say I had made my move that it was all too late, that I had even met another guy who I was starting to fall in love with, but before I had the chance to answer he kissed me and it just felt so good. Well, for a brief moment it did, until I looked up and saw Alberto standing at the front gate to Miss

Elaine's staring at me with a look of horror and sadness on his face! I couldn't believe it. I ran down the path to stop him getting back into the taxi he had just arrived in but bloody slipped on the fake snow, which by this stage had frozen solid, and fell arse over tit and landed on my face.

By the time I had got up Alberto was gone and so was Marcus, who must have realised I was seeing someone, and I was left with a fat lip and bleeding nose. I can't believe it, Suz: for years I have no one then two come along at once - and I bloody well stuff them both up!

I couldn't even enjoy the rest of Miss Elaine's party. My face, even with a frozen bag of peas on it, looked like Quasimodo and my dress ripped as I fell. I was indeed the real life Cinderella but left the party without a prince chasing after me.

When I arrived home I told Mum everything and had a good old cry. She wrapped me in a blanket, applied a new bag of peas to my face and gave me a hot chocolate and turkey sandwich. I was so glad I was close to home and Mum was there to comfort me. You must sometimes feel so far away from your parents, Suz. At least I can fly back home within a couple of hours but your folks are so far away. I hope you're spending plenty of quality time with them now, honey.

The day after Miss Elaine's party I went round to her 'Winter Wonderland' that had actually become an icy death trap after the fake snow had frozen over night. Apparently, three other guests had slipped over on their way out and someone told me the Vicar's wife had slipped into Miss Elaine's clipped bush! (Certainly made me chuckle!). Miss Elaine then told me how Alberto had got in touch with her after I told him I was going to be in the pantomime and that he wanted to come and see me on stage. He couldn't get time off work, though, so instead, Miss Elaine had invited him to the party as a surprise for me. She didn't know anything about Marcus though and was kicking herself for going behind my back. I told her not to be so silly, that it was the most romantic thing that had ever happened to me - and then I burst out crying again as I realised how much I liked Alberto and what an amazing guy I just lost. She then told me to buck up and that she'd come to visit me in Barcelona, where she'd help me find a new Spanish man and that she might find one for herself while she was at it.

151

So there you have it. Now what do I do, Suz? In two days time I return to Barcelona and instead of going back to a blossoming romance, I return to single life again. I tried phoning Alberto and sending him messages but he's not replied. I even sent Marcus a message explaining how sorry I was about not being completely honest and that I hoped I hadn't hurt his feelings but he hasn't replied either. Wish you were here, Suz. You'd know what to do.

Love,

Rachel xxx

Chapter 6
January – New Year's Resolutions

1st January

Dear Rachel,

It was so lovely having you home for Christmas. Your father and I haven't stopped talking about how proud we are of all your achievements so far. I mean, moving to a foreign country and learning the language is such a big task. Whenever I'm away with your father he uses hand gestures and ends up pointing at things.

Since you left we had a few days relaxing at home, eating turkey leftovers (Your father and I are convinced they are genetically modifying turkeys so they're bigger) and watching our favourite Christmas specials. Well I did anyway; your father mostly slept on the sofa in his new festive jumper and would wake up occasionally to eat some cheese and crackers. Talking of which, I ended up buying him a plastic baby bib from the local charity shop so he'd stop getting crumbs on my sofa! The lady in the shop said she didn't realise we had a baby in the family. Naturally, I had to lie and told her it was in preparation for when you had a baby and would be visiting in the future!

How is the love life, darling? I felt so upset for you after Miss Elaine's party. Has Alfonso been in touch? And how is your face, darling? Did the swelling and bruising go down in time for New Year? I bet you had a wild one. Your father and I stayed up until a minute past midnight to watch Big Ben strike 12 and for the firework display and then went to bed; we're too old for all that these days. I remember we once stayed up until 2 A.M. - that was the year your father added five red bulls to the New Year punch!

Anyway chin up, my love. Things will pick up in the New Year. I suggest you set yourself some New Year's Resolutions like your Mummy and Daddy. Here are ours:

Mummy's Resolutions:
1. *Have a life laundry and sort out the spare room.*
2. *Take up a new hobby.*
3. *Don't boss my dear husband around so much.*

Daddy's Resolutions:
1. *Listen more carefully to what my dear Wife tells me.*
2. *Clean out the crap from the garage and shed.*
3. *Take my dear Wife on more holidays and day trips.*

And before you say anything, yes, I did write your father's resolutions for him because if I didn't he wouldn't bother. In fact, darling, I'm going to add some for you as well. It's entirely up to you whether you take them up or not but I think they'd do you good - and Mother knows best.

Rachel's Resolutions:
1. *Start baking again.*
2. *Continue learning Spanish.*
3. *Continue writing letters to your dear old Mummy and your friends.*

Well, my darling, it's time I was heading off. Your father needs to start on his resolution number 2 and I'm in danger of breaking my resolution number 3 on the first day of the year!

Love, peace and happiness,

Mum and Dad xxx

P.S: I'm currently wearing my home-knitted jumper from Great Aunt Shelly. I think she might have got a bit confused with the pattern, though, as one sleeve is very long and the other is very short. The picture is also a little distorted - apparently, it's meant to be a black cat and a brown mouse sitting next to each other but your father says it looks like a cat sitting next to a large poo! How's your crocheted bikini? I bet you you'll be the trendsetter this summer on the beach!

3rd January

Dear Rach - you stupid dingbat, you!

How are you feeling? I've tried phoning and emailing but you're not answering so I'm resorting to sending you another one of my sickly sweet kitten cards from WHSmiths in an attempt to get a response.

I understand how you must feel, God knows the times I've cocked things up and felt alone. Things will work out, though, just give it time. I got back home yesterday and your Mum popped in to water my 'long-suffering plants'; she thought I was away for another few days. She told me how down you were and after reading your letter I can see why. Your Mum has some good advice, though, sweet cheeks: get busy! It's the best way to get over a man and seeing as you're getting over two of them (tramp) I suggest you do all three things on your recommended resolutions list ASAP or else I'll be out on the next plane to sort you out.

Now, as I've continued to write to you, you can do me a favour: bloody well pick up the phone and give me a ring as soon as you get this letter so I can tell you all about my Xmas in Oz. I'm willing to write to you a couple of times a month, honey, but I can't bloody write the epic essay's you scrawl off. So if you want to hear about my run-in with a shark and the hot lifeguard who saved me, you'd better get on the blower!

Love you, you silly moo!

Suz x

P.S: I'm off round Miss Elaine's to watch the DVD of the pantomime this afternoon. I've heard it should have an X rating after your busty performance! Let's hope she's not got a 3D television!

6th January

Dearest Rachel,

Happy New Year to you! I seriously hope you had a wonderful time and that you didn't let all that business with those men get you down. It's so not worth it, Rachel. My goodness, if I counted the hours over the years that I had spent pining over men, it would add up to years, I'm sure! Now to cheer you up, I've decided to come visit you over Easter - but more than that, I've booked us a couple of train tickets for a mini-break to Madrid while I'm there, and you're coming with me. Your Mum said you've not been and I've been in touch with that dreadful Madam Sanchez and managed to get you a week off work. If she asks, however, you are to say it is totally true that your sick and frail Aunt Clementine from Peru is making a visit and that you are taking her to a retreat for the afflicted. I'm not really sure why I invented such a complex story, I guess it's my dramatic side; anyway, she fell for it and we've got a mini-break to plan!

Suz came round yesterday and we watched the pantomime together with Rory and his dog. Had a super afternoon. I tell you what, we did pull it off; it was a super show. Mind you, we did get through three bottles of wine as we watched it so perhaps that made it slightly more entertaining than it actually was. I've decided to take a six month break from the Am Drams and will return in the summer to direct an Agatha Christie murder mystery. She tells a bloody good story and the local biddies love a 'Whodunnit?'

Off to play a round of golf now with a delightful fellow; the Lord of Latchington Manor. He came to the pantomime and was impressed by my direction, so he said. Invited me to a round of golf and spot of lunch in West Shillington so I thought I'd check out his swing. Nice to see I've not totally lost it, darling, and if there's hope for this old bird there's certainly hope for you too!

Much love,

Miss Elaine

Xxx

10th January

Dear Mum and Dad,

Thanks for the great advice, Mum. At first I cringed at the thought of doing New Year's Resolutions, as they usually fizzle out after a month and then only make me feel guilty for the next eleven months. But after having three motivational letters from Suz, Miss Elaine and yourself, as well as a long phone call from Suz, I have decided to embrace my New Year's Resolutions and have even embellished them!

Rachel's Resolutions:

1. Start baking again and set up my own business.
2. Continue learning Spanish and get to Stage 3.
3. Continue writing letters to my dear old Mummy and my friends.

Ok, so resolution number 1 seems quite a big one but you need to think big to make big things happen, am I right? I don't aim to do anything drastic and will continue working for the evil Madam Sanchez until I feel I can make a living for myself but at least, for now, I can start planning to do something new with my life, which was the whole reason I decided to move to Spain in the first place.

This morning I enrolled in Stage 2 of my Spanish course and I'm also determined to start making some Spanish friends. I was hoping I'd do that naturally through Alberto (not Alfonso, Mum!) but seeing as he's not around, I've also joined a group of Spanish/English people who want to practice conversations with each other in each other's language. I don't know what it will be like but think it's a positive step in the right direction.

And as for Resolution number 3, there's no danger of that one failing. I love my letter writing and besides it keeps my postman busy, which makes me feel like I'm contributing to Spanish employment.

Love to you both,

Rachel

P.S How are your resolutions going?

10th January

Dear Suz,

Thanks for the motivational talk, you old cow! I miss having you near. Can't wait 'til you visit next month. I can't believe I spent so long feeling sorry for myself. I missed celebrating New Year and Three Kings Day on the 6th as my face still looked like I'd been in the ring with Mike Tyson and I didn't feel like going out. I was invited to spend the evening with Lucy but I didn't want to inflict my moody self on her and her boyfriend. She's been great, though. I met up with her this week and told her all about it. She pretty much said the same as you guys and then when I showed her my list of resolutions, she told me that she also loved baking and wouldn't it be great to have a little café one day? At the time, we both fantasized and laughed but then a couple of days later it was still in my head. So we chatted again and she said that if we planned it properly she'd do it, she'd open up a traditional British Tearoom with me here in the heart of Barcelona. It sounds a bit bonkers and we're certainly not rushing into anything but the dream has been dreamt and now it's just down to us.

Anyway, that's still a long way off and I'm still

163

suffering the wrath of Madam Sanchez. Today she told me that I had put on a lot of weight over the Christmas holidays and that she was struggling to squeeze behind me at the front desk!!! Cheeky cow! Sad thing is she's right, though. I think I may have overindulged whilst staying at Mum and Dad's because my arse is looking huge. I have even been struggling to get to my flat on the top floor this week. My neighbour even asked to pass by me yesterday, and she is in her nineties! I think I'd better add a 4th resolution, the recurring resolution for the last 12 years: Go to the gym and lose weight! A resolution you'll never need on your list, you skinny cow. I guess it must be because of all the sex you have. I can't believe what you did with that poor lifeguard. And there he was thinking the shark was the man-eater!

Thanks for cheering me up honey, and thanks for writing to me. What I'd do without your sickening animal cards I don't know!

Love,

Rach xxx

12th January

Dear Rachel,

Happy New Year to you, I hope my letter finds you in good health. I heard that you were back in the village over the holidays. I even understand you had a 'starring' role in the local pantomime. If we had known, Kevin and I might have come. We don't usually do amateur theatre, though, as it so often disappoints and ruins the original source material. I guess panto is different, though, as its not real acting, more prancing around the stage being silly.

I'm just writing to say that Kevin and I have decided to visit Barcelona this year and thought we'd pop in on you at some point. We might come in March, as the weather won't be overly warm. I come out in the most terrible heat rash in warm weather and it just doesn't agree with Kevin. Which hotel do you work in? You didn't say in your last letter. I was thinking Kevin and I might stay there. We both said "wouldn't it be funny having you wait on us?"! Kevin even suggested we get a bell and ring for you when we wanted something. He's such a laugh!

Perhaps on your day off you could also take us around the city on a tour. I'm sure you know it quite well by now but don't worry if your language skills aren't up to it as Kevin has a GCSE in Spanish.

Kind regards,

Victoria

14th January

Dear Alberto,

I'm so sorry that your surprise journey to see me in England resulted in you seeing me kissing another man. I can't really make excuses for what you saw, as there are no excuses to give. I can, however, say that it wasn't planned and that I just felt a little confused at the time. And now I realise I am making excuses, even though I said I wouldn't, and I guess that's because I feel very sad that I hurt you. I'll understand if you don't want to see me again but I hope that perhaps you'll forgive me and maybe one-day we can be friends. I miss your company.

Love,

Rachel x

P.S If it helps, whilst running down the path to you I slipped and smashed my face in.

14th January

Dear Miss Elaine,

You really are the best! I can't believe you've organised a mini-break for me with a week off work too! When Madam Sanchez first told me about it I hadn't actually received your letter so must have come across as rather confused but then the more she explained the more I thought it could only possibly be one person who would create a plan like that. You are completely crazy! I can't wait to spend time with my Aunt Clementine from Peru! It's going to be so much fun!

How did the golf date go? I hope he knocked you for 6! (Is that a golfing reference or cricket?) I have a good feeling about this one. I can so imagine you with a Lord. You'd naturally have to be known as Lady Elaine instead of Miss Elaine, though, but I'm guessing you'd be O.K with that. I have just written to Alberto. Previously I had tried to call him but he wouldn't pick up so I wrote a letter instead. I'm not sure the words really summed up the way I felt or how much I want him back but at least I've made the effort. Will keep you updated...

Love,

Rachel xxx

P.S: I'll get us a guidebook to Madrid so we can
start planning a few places to visit. I can't wait!

16th January

Dear Rachel,

I should have never agreed to my third New Year's resolution. Every time I ask your father to do something he brings it up. I have to then tell I'm that I'm not bossing him around, I'm merely telling him what to do. Having said that, all the other resolutions are going well. I have well and truly sorted the spare room and packed up five large boxes for a car boot sale when the weather improves. There's nothing as depressing as a car boot sale in the rain so the boxes have been put into the newly organised garden shed ready for the first dry Sunday in February.

Your father has also managed successfully to take me on my first weekend away of the year! We donned our finest clothes, in fact, and went to Highclere Castle, where they film Downton Abbey, and took part in a theme weekend! It was your father's Christmas present to me after I took back the vastly overpriced and unrealistically optimistic underwear set he bought me, and in red, of all colours! No, a visit to Downton was much more my cup of tea - and plenty of cups of tea we had too. I was, after all, a Countess for the weekend and thoroughly enjoyed the attention from all of the servants (trained actors). Your father was a Lord and actually fitted into the role very well. He also liked the smoked salmon and cucumber sandwiches, which had their crusts cut off so they were extra posh!

The rooms were very plush indeed and I have to say I slept like a log. I didn't like it, however, when the maid came in while we were in bed to give us our morning tea. I'm sure many would have liked it but I hadn't even done my hair and your father was wearing his old PJ's instead of the ones I put out for him! All very embarrassing! I bet she went back and told all the other maids about it.

During the day we took part in various 'Downton Abbeyish' activities including a ride around the grounds in a classic car, a spot of croquet (your father hit the ball far too hard and almost hit a woman dressed as the Dowager Countess!) and, finally, an evening ball. I was given this amazing gown to wear - you would have loved it - and the music was very atmospheric. It was then that I decided what my second New Year's Resolution would be (a new hobby) and decided that I would audition for a role in Miss Elaine's summer production. I believe she's planning a period drama and after the weekend I had just had with your father I thought, why not? I could give it a go. I've never been on stage before and feel now that I'm approaching my 60's why not give a go. I know it's a way off but will keep you in the loop, darling.

Think I'm going to put my feet up this afternoon and watch a couple of repeats of Downton Abbey. I want to see if I can spot where we were standing in relation to Dame Maggie Smith.

Love, peace and happiness,

Mum and Dad xxx

P.S: For goodness sake write back to that awful Victoria Plum. I bumped into her as I was browsing the frozen desserts in the new Waitrose and she wouldn't let me go. On and on she went about her boring old husband Kevin and his allergies and how they were planning to come and visit you in Spain. I was there so long I thought I was going to catch hyperthermia from the cold!

18th January

Dear Gemma,

Hey honey, thanks so much for your letter last month. Don't worry about not writing sooner and I'm sorry too for not responding quicker! Life is busy and I certainly understand in your job how hard it must be in your job to have any free time at all, especially when you have Demon Child in your class! How's he been? I really hope he didn't ruin the Nativity for you.

I remember being in the Nativity; I was a shepherd. I desperately wanted to be an angel but I remember our evil class teacher Miss Rota telling me that I would be too chunky to be an angel. I wonder what happened to her; ooh, she was a bitter woman! Do you remember when she made us stand on our chairs because we glued our hands together because we were best friends? She must be about 100 now, if she's still alive; goodness, how many kids she traumatised over the years! Mum caught up with Mrs. Ashley the other day; now, she was a great teacher. I loved taking H.E with her. Do you remember that time she taught us how to make a loaf of bread? You added far too much yeast to yours and it

173

ended up being the size of a small elephant! I've not baked bread in ages! Think I might give it a go this weekend as part of my New Year resolutions; to bake more.

How were the Christmas holidays? Mum and Dad well? At least you get decent breaks throughout the year to recover from the class from Hell! It sounds like education has really changed over the last few years, though. I'm sorry that you're not enjoying it any more. You were always so full of life and ideas. Perhaps you just need a change of school or are all schools similar?

If you've haven't got any plans over the summer holidays, come and spend a week with me and we can moan about our jobs together! Would be lovely to have a good old catch-up. You'd so love it here, honey. The city is just full of things to do. Last weekend I visited Casa Batlló, which is one of the houses Gaudí designed here in Barcelona. Just knowing how much you love art, you would just adore it. His architecture is so imaginative and organic looking. Some parts of the house look like shells while other parts look like bones — but not in a gothic horror way, in a naturally beautiful way. My favourite part, however, was the rooftop; the tiles are decorated and shaped to form the body of a dragon and it's simply wonderful. I'm trying my best to use email as little as possible these days just because I feel in the past it ruled my life but I'll make an exception and email you some photos so you can see. If you do come in summer perhaps we can visit his other big house, La Pedrera, which is also in the same part of the city and is famous for it's incredible roof top and chimneys. There's normally a queue of a million tourists outside but if you book in advance you can usually skip the queues.

Hope this term goes better for you, honey. Chin up and remember there is nothing better for stress relief than wine, chocolate and a hot bubble bath! With my current job I have learnt to stock up and have a supply on demand for whenever the need arrives, which currently is about 3 times a week! I tell you, the sooner I escape from behind that reception desk, the better! I see life as triangle, one corner is work and the other two are family/friends and relationships. I currently have one corner I'm content with as I have just the best friends and family anyone could wish for but the other two corners are sadly missing. However, after a recent dive into wallowing in self pity

I am now working on corner number 2: work (I'm planning on starting up my own business). As for corner number 3: relationships, I've kind of mucked that one up a bit recently, so will leave that one for the time being and perhaps it will sort itself out!
I hope your triangle takes shape soon too, honey.

Love,

Rachel xxx

22nd January

Dear Victoria,

So lovely to hear from you again! My hotel is called The Barcelona Imperial and it would be a pleasure to have you and Kevin come to stay. Easter weekend is especially nice, I understand, and there's so much to do in the city at that time of year. Let me know what you decide.

Kind regards,

Rachel

22nd January

Dear Rach,

I can't believe we'll be celebrating carnival with you in one month! I am so excited, I just love a spot of dressing up. I've come up with all sorts of costume ideas for the three of us but as Suz and I will only have hand luggage, I think we'll get them in Barcelona. I've been online (it's something I know you don't really do that often, deary, you know on the computer thingy!) and found a fantastic fancy-dress shop 10 minutes from your flat, near Las Ramblas. I've also looked up a few gay bars, after all you girls need a night out with the gays.

Talking of gays, now that panto is over and done with for another year, my weekday nights are free so I thought it was time to start looking for Mr. Right again and think I've found him. "So soon?", I hear you say; well it all happened on New Year's Eve. I went to Brighton with my boys, Max and Jordi, and after dinner went to one of the gay bars on the front. Max, as usual picked up some muscled hunk and went off with a massive smile on his face and Jordi bumped into some of his Spanish friends. I swear to you Rach, there are more Spanish in Brighton than in Spain! They were all chatting away at a million miles an hour so I decided to pop outside for some fresh air - where I literally bumped into Mr. Right. He wasn't looking where he was going and walked right into me, causing me to spill my drink down myself, a bit like Julia Roberts did in Notting Hill, only I was looking more glamorous! He was ever so polite and immediately fetched some tissues and tried to help, then he offered to buy me another drink, which I gracefully accepted as he was so dishy. He's what we'd call a silver fox, honey, a bit of a George Clooney! Well, after he returned with a couple of drinks we ended up chatting for the rest of the night and then, as the clock struck midnight, we kissed and it just felt so right. Then when I finally caught up with the boys again, we swapped numbers and agreed to meet up for lunch a couple of days later.

Well, my lovely, since then I've seen him 6 times for lunches and dinners and anything revolving around food, really, as we are both right old foodies and it's just been wonderful. His name is Harry and he lives in a gorgeous flat overlooking the sea in Hove Actually. Best of all though, Rach, he loves dogs and has two of his own who get on really well with Mr. Paws.

It's amazing to think how quickly things can change, really. Max and Jordi are both over the moon for me, especially as Harry has cute friends that they can flirt with! Tomorrow we are having a picnic on the South Downs with the dogs, then on Friday I'm introducing him to Suz! I hope she likes him. I think you'd like him, honey; perhaps when you're back next you'll get to meet him! No more internet dating for me, this one's a keeper!

How's your love life, darling? Has Bertie been in touch yet? I still can't believe he came all the way over to see you. And equally so I can't believe the bloody bad timing of Marcus making a move on you, especially after all this time! Anyway chin up, honey, loving the idea of setting up your own business. I can so see you wearing a polka dot pinny (like your mum wears), standing behind the counter serving your amazing traditional English scones and tea to all those Spanish grannies. Have you told your Mum yet? Bet she's already making you a new batch of floral pinnies to wear!

Hugs and kisses,

Rory and Mr. Paws xxx

24th January

Dear Mum & Dad,

Or should I be addressing you as Lord and Lady Williams, now that you've been to Downton Abbey?! Glad you had a fun time. Sounds like a wonderful experience and just your cup of Earl Grey tea! I'm currently watching the 3rd series so a bit behind you, so no spoilers, please! Heaven forbid I find out Maggie Smith loses it and blows them all up in series 4!

Talking of old women who defy their actual age and live a more active life than most young people I know (including myself!), I saw my neighbour Belen at the swimming pool this week. It was actually a very funny story; one that I'm sure will really make you laugh. So I turned up at my gym and decided that instead of falling off the rowing machine or tripping on the running machine, I'd go for a swim. This is all part of the New Year health plan after Madam Sanchez suggested quite rudely (unfortunately correctly, though) that I had put on weight over Christmas. I therefore got changed into my enormous swimsuit (think Victorian bathing costume) and headed to the pool. Once there I started to do my lengths of the pool. After 5 minutes, though, all the local old biddies, including Belen, arrived to do an aqua aerobics class on the other side of the pool. This was all well and good as it's a large pool; however, the instructor, standing on the pool edge, asked the twenty or so old ladies to rotate in a large circle around the pool. At first this was fine and I carried on with my lengths whilst observing how much they looked like those manatees from under the water. Large, bobbing creatures who were circling around the pool about to perform tricks. The things was, though, that the power of twenty large women circling the pool started to create quite a current and before the instructor realised what was happening and could get them to reverse direction, a whirlpool effect had been created and the women started to whizz round, crashing into each other. The current then became so strong that myself and three other swimmers from the swimming lanes were also pulled into this massive vortex of woman and the next thing you know, I'm circling the pool with my face pressed up against Belen's ample cleavage! The other swimmers, meanwhile, were spinning between the biddies' legs and one daring granny who wore a two piece bikini soon regretted that as she lost it and span round the pool topless for all the old men in the jacuzzi to see! Oh Mum, it was hysterical. Well, not exactly right at that moment in time but eventually when the water returned to normal and we all started laughing. Belen gave me a big hug and said something about me joining them next time but I'm not really sure I'm up to it to tell the truth! Those women are inspirational. Ever thought about aqua aerobics as your new hobby, Mum?

I'm impressed with your decision to try a spot of acting. If you do go through with it I will definitely come back to see you perform. It might actually be the next time I visit as I'm not going to be back at Easter as I thought I would; instead, Miss Elaine and I are going to Madrid for a long weekend! I don't know if she told you but we're going to go on the high-speed train from Barcelona and then stay in a gorgeous hotel in the centre of the city. Can't wait! I've been hoping to see more of Spain, so this is a great opportunity. I was told there's so much to do there and that Easter is especially nice, as it's not too hot. I'm particularly looking forward to having a hot chocolate with churros (a bit like long doughnuts) in one of the famous cafes there. I feel a bit sad that I won't be doing it with Alberto but I guess it wasn't meant to be.

You will be pleased to know though that I am immersing myself in my resolutions and keeping very busy, which is a very good thing indeed. I think I take after you, Mum!

Love, peace and happiness,

Rachel xxx

P.S You'll be pleased to know I have responded to blooming Victoria Plum so you should be safe for a while. I do suggest, though, that you carry a large fly swat around with you at all times and if she tries to corner you in the freezer aisle again, you swat her!

28th January

Dear Rach,

I can't believe I've had the time to write back to you so soon but your last letter inspired me and gave me a much needed kick up the bum. I've been such a drip lately and your offer to visit you over summer put a smile on my face and gave me a boost of positivity I've not had in quite some time.

Yes, the kids are still crazy and the Head is still an uptight cow but when you reminded me of being in Miss Rota's class, I suddenly thought that if I carried on as I had been going, I would end up like her; a bitter, negative old fart. I know that for sure, too, as I went to a training day a month ago and she was there. Can you believe she's still teaching at the same school and is as crabby as ever! Every time the trainer suggested something she huffed and puffed and just came out with all this negativity and after you mentioned her in your letter I suddenly had a vision of being just like her in the future. I then pictured Mrs. Ashley and thought about what a positive influence she had on all our lives and decided to make a change.

I took your advice and had a hot bath, then settled down to watch Dirty Dancing with a glass of wine and a box of chocs and suddenly felt much better. Then, the following day I went into school with a smile on my face, a spring in my step and took back my personal power. The rest of the week was hard at times and I think the other teachers thought I was on drugs but I felt so much better. I've also decided that this weekend I'm going to look for another job. You were completely right; either I change schools and find one that makes me feel valued again or I find a totally different job. For the record, I think your business idea is wonderful. You were always amazing at baking and from the sounds of things your new friend Lucy will make the perfect business partner. If you need me to test any cake recipes when I visit, I'd gladly help!

Your dear friend,

Gemma xxx

P.S: For your information Demon Child was off sick for the Nativity so it was a great success. He did however tip a pot of red paint all over the class guinea pig last week!

30th January

Dear Rachel,

I'm sorry I've taken so long to reply to your letter and I know you also tried to call me but I was upset and confused. When I saw you kissing someone else I felt stupid for coming to the UK and for presuming we had developed something more that it obviously was. We Spanish are very passionate people and also very stubborn; we often think with our hearts before we use our heads. I've had time to think however and realise that we never said we were actually in a relationship and that you should be free to kiss whoever you like. I must admit, though, that I wanted to be the person kissing you. Of course I want to be your friend but hope you really want to be more than friends. I do not know, however, how you feel about the incredibly handsome man I saw you with at Christmas, therefore will let you decide. If you'd like to meet for a coffee soon – let me know.

Alberto x

P.S: If I had realised you had fallen I would have come to help you up.

Chapter 7
February – The Carnival Queen

1st February

Dear Suz,

He's written, Suz; Alberto has got in touch and I'm
half filled with hope and love and happiness and the
other half guilt and sadness that I made him feel so
bad. He wants to meet for a coffee and says he
hopes we can be more than friends. I realise I'm
going to have to build up the trust we had together
but am now clear what I want and I know that it's
him. Marcus Flynn had his chance, I'm no longer even
in the UK and even though I find him attractive, he's
not the man for me. However, I don't want to hurt
Alberto again so have decided to take things slowly.
Sometimes I feel I've had so much change in the
last year that perhaps something a little less
complicated and more straightforward is needed. Oh
well, we'll see. I'm going to suggest meeting him this
weekend so will let you know how it goes. Any advice
would be appreciated!

Love,

Rach xxx

3rd February

Dear Rory,

I always knew you'd end up with a silver fox. Having said that I didn't always know it would a man. Do you remember back to secondary school when you were obsessed by Angela Lansbury and 'Murder She Wrote'! I even remember you having a picture of her in your study bay in Sixth Form! I should have guessed you were gay and not into older women though! The signs were all there; the obsession with Cher, the admiration you showed for Jake Ham the captain of the football team.... You always said you were impressed by his ball skills, well, that I now believe!

Your foxy daddy sounds lovely, though, and it's great that he's also a dog lover. What type of dogs does he have? I'd love to have one but I'm not sure a tiny flat on the 7th floor is really a suitable place for one. Send me a pic of Harry so I can check him out. What does he do? I'm picturing antiques dealer.

My love life is a little complicated after the Christmas kiss fiasco but at least Alberto has agreed to see me now. I'm seeing him in two days for coffee and am working myself up into a right old mess. I mean, do I kiss him as I had been doing before, shake his hand? I'm not sure if I should apologise again or defend myself and say that Marcus kissed me first. Anyway as Doris Day would say "Que sera sera".

I'm happy you're so excited about carnival. I've heard it's great. For the past few weeks I've been going to my Stage 2 Spanish Classes and my weekly language exchange gathering and have been learning much more about all the local festivals and celebrations. I've teamed up with a nice Spanish girl named Maria in my exchange group and she's been telling me all about local places to go to, parties to attend and restaurants to try. She's a bit of a party animal and I'm not sure I'd be able to keep up with her but I'm certainly willing to give it a go. She was telling me all about Sitges carnival and said the best time to go was the Sunday night, as we can watch the parade and then celebrate in the streets afterwards. She also said we can either get the train back to Barcelona at 4am in the morning or get a room in a hotel. I'm sure that when I was in my 20's, I'd say train but after chatting to Suz, we've both agreed to get a room for the night. It's got three single beds so I hope you don't mind but I have booked it up, as it was the last one left. That way we can party all night but then have a bit of comfort once we've worn our heels out!

Maria has also recommended a fab place for dinner that specialises in local fish dishes and also a trip to the Bacardi Museum! Did you know the man who invented Bacardi rum came from Sitges? I have a feeling it was destiny us all going there!

Hope your pooch is being a good boy. Who's looking after him while you're away? I'm sure Mum and Dad would take him for you. Dad needs to get some exercise and he was always so good with Bertie when we had him. OMG! I've just realised our family dog had the same name as the guy I'm seeing/not seeing/about to see - Alberto - Bertie! It must be a sign! Can't believe I didn't spot it earlier. Hee, hee!

Love and hugs,

Rach xxx

5th February

Dear Rachel,

So lovely to chat to you the other day darling, I do miss you being around. I know your father and the old biddies at the flower club take up lots of my time but I still miss my number one girl. I know you said you'd love us to visit in May and we're very keen to do so; you don't think it will be too much for you, darling? I mean, you already have so many visitors booked in. If it helps, your father and I will book a hotel nearby, that way you don't have to give your bed up for us, and your father doesn't need to climb the 7 floors of stairs. He's not as agile as he used to be and even though your neighbour is 93 and much older, I just think it may be a little too much for him. Having said that, if you can squeeze us in for a spot of sight seeing and other bits and bobs, we'd be delighted to come and see you.

In other news, we had a very special Flower Club this week where we teamed up with the Camera Club. And before you ask, yes, I did get a few funny looks from their members after your father exhibited that topless picture of me last year. The evening started off pleasantly enough with a talk from their Chairman, Tom, Gill's husband, about photography of plants and gardens in the local area but it soon went downhill when he showed us a PowerPoint presentation of a project he had in mind to raise money for a local charity. The PowerPoint presentation consisted of pictures of the Women's Institute Calendar Girls with nothing on apart from a smile and a couple of buns covering their modesty. Apparently, he got the idea after seeing my photo and thought the women of the Flower Club would be interested in helping him out. Well, as you can imagine there was uproar; we even had a couple of ladies storm out (when I say storm I mean shuffle, and not even very quickly as they both had walking sticks!) I tried to calm the situation and suggested we break for tea and buns!

After the break, thankfully, we had a gardening expert who defused the situation and the change of topic proved to do the trick. Both groups were interested and the evening was brought to a civil end. Once everyone had gone, though, I just had this nagging feeling about why Tom had suggested such a thing and he told me that Gill had been diagnosed with cancer just before Christmas. He told me my photo had reminded me of the Calendar Girls film and how they raised money for a cancer charity, too, and that he thought it was a good way of raising awareness and making money for the charity. He said he just wasn't very good at public speaking and that he still found it very hard to explain to others that his wife had cancer.

I was totally speechless and then said I'd do it. I said I'd find eleven other ladies - maybe not from the Flower Club, after their reaction to the proposal - but that I'd do it. I mean, it would be done tastefully, I'm sure, but if Dame Helen Mirren and the Ladies from the W.I can do it, then so can I. So, darling, if I can't find eleven volunteers here I'll be asking a favour of you! I know it's a bit daring but Gill is such a kind and gentle women. All those years she taught you in school and when you were growing up, she and Tom would babysit you, too. I think that,

195

because she never had any children of her own. she thought of you a bit like the daughter she never had. She's the reason you can bake so well, that's for sure! I just can't believe she kept it to herself. I just wish she had told someone about it.

The next day I went round to see her. Tom hadn't told her what he was up to and at first she was rather cross with him but I explained to her that it was his way of doing something, something positive and not only for Gill but for other women like her too. At first she apologised that Tom had suggested such a 'daring' way of raising money but when I told her that I'd already agreed to do it, she laughed and after a while, said she'd better volunteer herself then, too. It was the right thing to do, wasn't it darling? I just kept thinking if that had been me, what would I have wanted people to do? Your father said the same thing. In fact, he's offered to take all the photos!

Love, peace and happiness,

Mum and Dad xxx

P.S: Do you think Miss Elaine and Suzy would take part?

P.P.S: We are still laughing about what happened to you in the swimming pool. Every time they mention swimming on the T.V or show a swimming pool we both crack up! We take it you won't be going back at the same time next week!

7th February

Dear Suz,

Just got back from a five-hour coffee session with Alberto and I'm very pleased to say things are good between us; actually things are very good. Basically, I started by just telling him everything that had happened and how I was feeling and how sorry I was and he simply stopped me and kissed me. Naturally, I kissed him back and he said that what was in the past was behind us and if I wanted, we could start over. I responded by kissing him. He then teased me, saying if that was starting over then, I just kissed him on the mouth before even introducing myself. We then spent the following hour reintroducing ourselves, all the while teasing each other. He even wickedly reminded me that since we had only just met he could finally forget about Halloween and the green face paint incident that he said haunted him for the following month!

I tell you what, Suz; I'm so lucky I met him and feel even luckier that he's given me a second chance. He did, however, want to know all about Marcus and so I told him. He then told me that he wasn't surprised that so many men were fighting for my attention, as I was so beautiful, when my face wasn't bright green!

We then spent the rest of the afternoon walking around the city and as it was cold - yes, Suz, it can get cold here so tell Rory not to pack only vest tops and hot pants! - he put his arm round me and held me close. We then bid each other farewell, as sleeping together on a 'first' date wouldn't be right. We'd wait until the second!

I'm seeing him again on Valentines Day when he's coming round for dinner. I'm going to cook him a special meal and dish him up one of the new desserts I've been practicing. Perhaps if things continue to go well you'll be able to meet him when you visit.

Lots of love,

Rach xxx

P.S: You've been awfully quite on the 'dating' front since you got back from Oz. What's going on?

12th February

Dear Rach,

You lucky cow! How on earth have you found such an amazing man? I can't believe the way he responded, so grown up and understanding. Not at all like the little boys I seem to end up with. I can't wait to meet him now, see if he's got a single friend he can match me up with! This time next year I foresee a wedding and, naturally, I will be your chief bridesmaid; just don't make me wear pink! Well, now things are back on track with Bertie, don't go bloody kissing any more long lost admirers and complicate matters again!

My love life is barren, darl, yet I'm surrounded by loved-up couples! Rory is besotted with his sugar daddy, Harry, and rightly so, as he's divine, Miss Elaine has been on several dates now with her Lord Snooty, who I've yet to meet and now you're back with your hot chorizo! Worst of all, it's coming up to that most dreaded of dates, Feb 14th, Valentine's Day! Do you remember all those anti-valentine dinners we had round your flat eating ice-cream, bitching about guys and watching chick flicks in our PJ's? Well, I might be doing that again this year, only on my own!!! Not that I want you to feel too guilty, just a little bit. Even Fat (only not fat anymore) Janet has a boyfriend! Perhaps I'd better join the nunnery and be done with!

Before I become a nun, however, I'd better complete the topless calendar girl photo shoot that your mad mother has convinced me to do, otherwise Mother Superior won't let me join! My goodness, Rach, your Mum does surprise me sometimes but always in the best possible ways. I was a bit shocked at first but then thought, why not, especially as it's for such a good cause. Poor Mrs. Ashley; I never took her class but she was always friendly and she was a star to you while you were growing up. Cancer is such a bloody bitch! I did try and convince your Mum to organize a sponsored fun run instead but she said she's never run anywhere in her life and wasn't going to start now; besides, she told me, she had already planned the themes for each month. Apparently I'm going to be Miss June because I've still got a good tan from my holidays to Oz. Your Mum is going to be Miss December and is hoping for a snow day so she has a wintery background. I'm not sure who the other ten women are, though, or if she'll even get another ten, you know how prudish some of the locals can be. Still, if anyone can organize it, your Mum can!

Lots of love,
Suz xx

14th February

Dear Mum and Dad,

Happy Valentines! I hope you two lovebirds are doing something nice to celebrate. I'm cooking dinner for Alberto tonight as we are now seeing each other again! (Does happy dance round the kitchen, bangs knee as kitchen is so small!). I'm making a homemade French onion soup with gruyere cheese croutons as a starter, followed by pan fried duck with crushed potatoes, green beans and a cherry sauce and then for pudding, I'm making a white chocolate and passion fruit cheesecake. As you always say, Mum, the quickest way to a man's heart is through his stomach! Hopefully that saying won't let me down tonight!

I'm afraid I can only do a quick letter today as I'm going to be cooking up that treat 'Nigella style' for the rest of the day; but I had to write and congratulate you on your bravery and kindness, Mum, for organizing the Calendar Girls photo shoot. I think it's such a good way to make money and raise awareness for the cause. I'm also sure that both Tom and Gill really appreciated it. How's Mrs. Ashley doing? What type of cancer has she got? She was the best teacher I've ever had and more than that, really. Whenever I needed support in school I'd go to Mrs. Ashley and she'd be there with tons of good advice. Her baking tips were also the best and you're certainly right, Mum, she's the reason I can bake, which means she's the one who is helping me escape my current nightmare job and set up my own business. If you need me to help out, Mum, I'll gladly do so. Keep me fully up to date and tell Dad to keep his eyes on the lens and nowhere else!

Love you both,

Rachel xxx

16th February

Dearest Rachel,

Congratulations on salvaging the relationship with Mr. Barcelona. He seemed such a nice chappy whilst we were corresponding about his surprise trip over to see you. I'm so glad that you're both giving it a second chance. Talking of second chances, it seems like there's more chances in this old dog than I even thought! If I'm honest, Rachel, I kind of thought that the whole 'dating' game was over for me but it seems like I was wrong. Robert - or if I should use his full title, Lord Robert George Warren - has rather swept me off my feet. The past couple of weeks have been a flurry of picnics, walks, day trips and dinners. He's a couple of years older than me but like me; full of beans. He owns Latchington Manor House but currently lives in a gorgeous cottage in the grounds as the House itself is now a museum for the public to look round, not that anyone does, according to Robert. He's not at all like a Lord, though, and his down-to-earth charm is what first attracted me to him. He's certainly very generous, though, and spoils me rotten. He's asked if I want to invite any friends to look round the Manor and the gardens next week, as they have just completed renovations with a plan to re-launch the place, so I'm inviting your Mum and Dad. I just know your Mum will love the gardens and even though it's still winter, the grounds are delightful. Your Dad will also have a field day taking photos for his Camera Club.

Talking of Camera Club, I've naturally said I'll take part in the Calendar Girls project but have insisted I have my photo taken last so that I have an extra few weeks to tone up. Not that a couple of weeks will make a difference but still I need to attempt to get the bingo wings, as you always call them, under control. Why the human body decides to sudden droop in all the wrong places I really don't know. It's not like we're not using it in the same way. In fact, in recent weeks, I've been using it in ways I've not attempted since my 20's!

Chow for now darling,

Miss Elaine xxx

P.S: Your Mum had been telling me your idea about you setting up your own business instead of working for that awful Madam Sanchez. I think it's a terrific idea; those frosted cupcakes you made for my Christmas Party were divine. If you need a bit of a financial boost and a silent partner let me know, darling, as I'd be more than happy to help.

18th February

Dear Rachel,

I'm so glad you think I did the right thing taking a lead with the Calendar Girls Project. It's had a slight theme change in the last few days but is still going full steam ahead despite some disapproving looks and comments from some of the village gossips and doom mongers. We had a little meeting two nights ago and Gill sensibly brought up the issue of making a calendar with the calendar year having actually already started. We chatted about making it and releasing it for next year but then Tom rightly stated that we should aim to make us much money as possible as soon as possible as there were people suffering right now. Then Suz had a brainwave; she explained how we were writing letters to you and how lots of people still enjoyed writing letters so we should make a series of themed cards. That way it also didn't matter if we had 12 women or not as we could just produce a set of cards to sell. Everyone agreed and then we each were allocated jobs to do. Here's the list:

Tom: Publicity – call the local paper, look for shops to promote or even sell the cards, go on the local radio…
Your Father: Printing cards (Wanted to be photographer but I wouldn't let him!!) He's got old contacts with friends in the printing world so I told him now was the time to refresh those contacts.
Your Mother: Events organiser & Model
Suz: Publicity – Look for local sponsors & Model
Andy: Camera Man (Lovely young man from the camera club and

according to Tom the best photographer in the club.)
Models: Fat Janet, Tammy from the flower shop, Felicity (Fairy Godmother before Miss Elaine took over) - she felt she missed out on the fun of the panto as she had the flu so was happy to be part of this; Miss Elaine, Gill (if she feels up to it) and finally you, my dear. I'm hoping we get a few more volunteers in the next few days but for now we have enough to get started.

Next week we're going to start planning a theme for each photo; cheeky, but at the same time classy - we don't want it looking like some cheap filth, after all. Then the following week, we'll shoot the photos followed by one further week where the cards will be edited and sent off to be made up. In a strange way it's exciting but at the same time filled with sadness, I have to keep reminding myself why we're doing it, after all, and it's because Gill has ovarian cancer and we're trying to save her and other women like her. Apparently it's more common in women who are over 50 but other than that, there doesn't seem to be any significant reason why she's developed it, as it doesn't run in the family. She's currently recovering from her second lot of chemotherapy and doesn't look at all well but her spirits are high, as you'd expect. She has always been a positive person and I think that's making her fight it. I'm really not sure how much money we'll make but I guess we're doing something about it and that's why Tom came to us in the first place.

Love, peace and happiness,

Mum and Dad xxx

P.S: How did the Valentine's dinner go? Sounded delicious. Tonight we're having beans on toast at your father's insistence. I'm predicting a windy night ahead!

24th February

Dear Mum and Dad,

Valentine's dinner wasn't exactly how I imagined it would be but despite what can only be described as 'bloody cock ups' along the way, it all ended well! So after writing to you last time I popped to the post box and posted your letter, and then went to the local market and got all the things I needed to cook dinner and returned home. After lugging all my shopping up the seven flights of stairs, I realized I had bloody forgotten to get the duck! Quite a vital ingredient if you're planning on making pan-fried duck! So I left everything, went back to the shops, bought the duck, climbed back up the seven flights of stairs and started to prepare the dishes only to discover my dear 'el flato' had no electricity!! By this stage, as you can imagine, I was on the verge of a nervous breakdown so went round to Belen's flat to check on her electricity, to find hers was working fine and that it was apparently a recurring fault with my flat. The landlord insisted it would be fixed but I'd have to wait until the following day to have it done. I was near to ringing Alberto to change plans and go out to dinner when Belen kindly suggested I cook it in her 'el flato', then simply take the food through to mine and have a romantic candle lit dinner in the dark. In fact, she pretty much insisted so I prepared all the food in her kitchen and when Alberto came over, with a huge bouquet of roses, dinner was ready and smelt amazing.

I only had one final worry, though, and that was the fact that I had used Belen's kitchen, she had helped me and whilst I cooked she decorated my flat and I was about to leave her on her own as I ate all the food with my date. My problem was soon solved, however, as Alberto sensing my concern, split the bouquet of roses in two, gave half to me and the other half to Belen, then insisted Belen join us for dinner. She tried to resist but we both insisted and we shared the meal out three ways in my candle-lit flat. I would never have imagined celebrating Valentine's with my 93 year old neighbour, but it was, in fact, the most wonderful evening. She entertained us with stories from her life and Alberto amused us with his charm and jokes and my food was the centre-piece to a most memorable evening.

After desert - which by the way was bloody marvellous - Belen then left us and Alberto and I enjoyed the rest of the evening talking until the final candle went out.

Since then we've been out another few times and hopefully this weekend I'll introduce him to Suz and Rory as they're coming to visit for the next four days! It's sure to be filled will plenty of events, so will fill you in next week.

Love you,

Rachel xxx

P.S Can you send me Mrs. Ashley's address, Mum, so I can send her a card. I just want to let her know I'm thinking of her.

28th February

Dear Miss Elaine,

Well, as expected, carnival weekend in Sitges was wild – and having both Rory and Suz here made it even more so. We started the weekend calmly enough by going for a walk round the neighbourhood so the guys could see where I lived. However, we soon found a little mojito bar which Rory insisted we went to so to celebrate their arrival after what sounded like a rather bumpy flight from Gatwick. Apparently the turbulence was so bad Rory screamed that they were all going to die, which caused panic and the children around him started to cry. Suz, on the other hand, said there was one slight bump, which didn't even knock over her gin and tonic!

Anyway, they arrived in one piece and it was so good to see them both. The one mojito turned into three, though, and by 9.30pm we were already a bit tipsy. After that Rory insisted we go to a local gay bar that he had looked up online and we ended up there until it closed. At one point, Suz was dancing on the bar, thinking she was Britney Spears – that was until she lost her balance and fell off. Luckily for her, she landed in the arms of her own hot Spanish guardian angel called Angel. Unfortunately for her, however, he had a boyfriend called David. Still, we had a whole heap of fun and I think I might even go back there with my friend Lucy sometime.

The following day after a much needed lie-in and brunch at Café Federal, a wonderful restaurant nearby that specializes in all things brunch, we made a mad dash for the fancy dress shop and, after trying on what seemed like 100 costumes, found some suitably spectacular feathered and sequined outfits. The heels were incredibly uncomfortable and not at all suitable but Rory insisted that if he were able to wear them, so would we. Yes, he dragged up. In fact, his legs looked better in the fishnet stockings than ours did! We soon packed up our fab new costumes and headed to Sitges, which is only 45mins on the train. Then we checked into our hotel and spent a couple of hours getting ready and having a few drinks to give us a little Dutch courage – after all it takes a certain amount of bravery to wear a highly camp sequined and feathered carnival costume in public – not that Rory seemed to let it bother him. I guess after so many years of going out in Brighton, he felt at ease! My fears were soon laid to rest, however, as everyone was dressed up. The streets were just packed with people in amazing outfits and the atmosphere was just electric. It was like a mini Rio de Janeiro on Carnival night. There were hundreds of floats, samba bands, carnival dancers... it was just terrific.

Everyone loved our costumes and we even got invited to ride on one of the floats, as some of their dancers hadn't turned up. Oh, Miss Elaine, if you could have seen us on top of this float surrounded by people, it was something I will never forget. Rory was most definitely the star, though; with his diamante heels and golden feathers, he really was the Carnival Queen. Suz and I looked stunning, too, in bright Barbie pink and canary yellow; however, we were a bit offended when someone asked to have their photo with the best drag queens in the entire parade! Bloody cheek! I told him we were real women but I'm not sure he believed us!

After the parade had finished we headed to the main street and we were fortunate enough to find a table at a bar, so we could take our heels off for half an hour and get a well deserved cocktail. Suz and I looked rather ruffled by this stage with sore feet and, despite the cold weather, sweat patches from dancing so much to the samba band. Rory, meanwhile, kept his heels on and still looked a million dollars. Then whilst we sat having our second mojito, Alberto spotted us and ran over. He was with his friends, all dressed as gangsters and, I have to say, he looked incredibly sexy. He had slicked his hair back and added a cute stick on moustache. They then joined us and shared their carnival stories with us. Alberto had spotted us earlier in the parade and had to look twice as he couldn't quite believe his eyes. For the rest of the night we then all went round the various bars together and it was so nice to see him getting on so well with Suz and Rory. Rory flirted terribly in his alter ego, Miss Sandy Spangle, but we all laughed a lot.

Finally, Suz and I couldn't take the heels any more and we called it a night. Alberto kissed me goodnight, losing his moustache in the process, so it ended up on my face – and then he cheekily told me to save the costume for a private performance later in the week! He then headed back to Barcelona on the train with his fellow gangsters as we happily stumbled the few streets to our hotel, where we collapsed into a heap of feathers and sequins and slept very well indeed.

The next couple of days were really nice too. We

spent time walking round the city, I showed the guys some of the hidden gems of the city which I like to visit and then the rest of the time we mostly ate and drank. This week I'm definitely on a detox and will not be drinking alcohol for some time!

On their final night we went out for dinner and Alberto, Lucy and my friend Maria from my Spanglish Class came too. I was a bit nervous whether everyone would get on but they did, and it was great to see Lucy and Suz hit it off, as I was afraid Suz might have thought I was replacing her with Lucy, especially as we're also going into business together. My concerns were unfounded though and the whole night was a success. The only trouble now is that I miss them. Having them here was so good and seeing how they fitted into my Barcelona life so naturally was just perfect; now they're gone, though, I kind of have a gap in my life. Silly, I know, as they're not far away but I miss them nonetheless.

Anyway, Missy, I'm not writing just to tell you about the madness of Carnival but also to thank you for your kind offer to help fund my business idea. I'm planning on having a very quiet March and have dedicated time to spend with Lucy, so that we can put together a detailed proposal and business plan. Once we have that in shape I'll send it your way and then perhaps we can plot our way forward from there. I so appreciate your faith in me, Miss Elaine; your friendship means so much.

Love,

Rachel xxx

Chapter 8
March – The Car Boot Queen

1ˢᵗ March

Dear Rachel,

Well, we finally had a sunny Sunday after a month of grey skies and minus temperatures, so your father and I decided to brave the cold and head to the car boot sale. I really don't mind the cold weather if the skies are clear, and thankfully, they stayed that way the entire day. Goodness knows, car boot sales are awful enough without the hindrance of dreadful weather!

We set the alarm for the crack of dawn and loaded the boxes into the car. I had packed them up the night before and though tempted to price-tag things, decided to let people make me an offer. We then had a quick breakfast and headed to the Library car park where the car boot was being held. Some spotty boy ushered us in and wanted us to park in a rubbish position, so I instructed your father to ignore him, and we set up in a terrific spot. The spotty boy said we had to move but I told him we needed more space due to my bad back and he soon scooted off. Then the worst bit came, the moment all car booters dread, the moment you open the car boot and bloody collectors and bargain hunters start rummaging through your stuff before you've even got out the car. One woman in particular was straight in there the moment your father clicked the open button. I was prepared for them, however, and had a water pistol to hand. I told them all to come back in 5 minutes, once it had all been unpacked or I'd squirt them in the face. Most backed off but some still ignored me so I sprayed them all with water. That soon got their attention and they shuffled off to the car that had just pulled in next to ours. *Bloody cheek! I tell you what, darling, I'd rather a genuine customer get a bargain on my stall rather than any of those people. I've been told they buy the best bits then go home and flog them on ebay and make a profit on it. Disgusting!*

The morning went quite quickly and I was pleased to sell most of the bits and bobs your father and I no longer wanted or needed. I was especially over the moon when I got £10 for a ghastly necklace I had been given for Christmas one year by some distant relative. I was, however, also caught out big time when along came Veronica Vase (ex chairwoman from Flower Club), who stopped to have a chat about the Calendar Girls project and other things, when I noticed on the table right under her nose was a wild strawberry scented candle set she had given me the previous Christmas. There was nothing I could do about it so tried to make out I was super busy with a customer who had been deciding for about 10 minutes whether or not to part with 20p for a egg cup. Finally she went and as she did so, complemented me on my perfume, she asked if it was some kind of berry! I smiled, then as soon as she had turned her back, grabbed the candle set and shoved it back in the car boot. I'm not entirely sure whether she spotted it or not but I certainly learnt my lesson.

By the end of the morning we had cleared most of the table and had made £110.59, not too bad at all. The leftovers - including the candle set - will go to one of the local charity shops next week as I certainly won't be doing another car boot for a while. As for our takings, I think we're going to buy a new bench for the garden. Your dad and I do like to sit in the garden over the summer and since chopping down the dreadful pampas grass, we have the perfect spot to now put it.

Calendar Girls update 1: As we're not actually making a calendar we can't really call ourselves the Calendar Girls, so from now on we're known as the Postage Pinups, as we're making cards to be posted to loved ones.

Postage Pinups update 2: We've now come up with a theme for each of the photos and are in the midst of collecting suitable props. Actually I found a wonderful old-fashioned watering can at the car boot that was perfect for one of the shots. We've decided, even though we're making cards and not a calendar, still to do shots based on the seasons/themes of the year. That way, if you're writing to someone in October, you can send the Halloween themed card or, in December, the Christmas-themed card etc. Here's the list of ideas:

Spring
Tammy – Watering Can shot (She's the village florist so perfect theme)
Gill – Some large Easter buns (She's going to make them twice as big as normal)

Summer
You – Beach shot (We thought your Alberto could take some pics of you on the beach in Barcelona and email them to us)
Suzy – Beach ball and paddling pool

Autumn

Fat Janet — Fireworks (Not real ones, Andy the camera man says he can add them in afterwards.)

Felicity— Halloween Pumpkin (She insisted she had something large to cover up her muffin top!)

Winter

Miss Elaine — Open fire toasting marshmallows (Apparently Latchington Manor House has the perfect fireplace and that Lord Robert has given us permission to shoot any of the photos there if we need to.)

Me — Snowman (The forecast says it's going to snow next week so we are hoping to build a snowman so I can 'peek' out behind it!

So there we have it. I'm hoping there's enough of a range there and that people will actually buy the cards once we've made them all. Your father has secured a company to print the cards for free, though, and the local paper is coming to interview us next week! I visited Gill yesterday and despite feeling very weak after her latest chemo sessions, she was in good spirits. I've enclosed a card with her address on it, darling, I'm sure she'd love to hear from you.

Love, peace and happiness,

Mum and Dad xxx

P.S Have you sorted out the electricity in your flat? Your father and I were very impressed with how kind you were to invite your old neighbour round for dinner with you and Alberto on Valentine's. He does indeed sound like a charming young man. I'm having a coffee with Suzy this week so will hear all about him and Carnival too. I understand feathers and sequins were involved!

5th March

Dear Rach,

My goodness, Sitges Carnival was amazing; seeing your flat was amazing; and meeting your gorgeous man was amazing! Rory and I just had the best time - but this week has been hell. It feels like we must have had a combined total of 2 hours sleep and at least 1000 units of alcohol over the entire weekend and then going back to work this week has been the pits. I don't regret it for a minute, though, as it was the most fun I've had in ages - in fact it was the most fun I've had since you bloody well left me to live in beautiful Barcelona.

It was so good to see you so set up and happy. I know your flat is a bit on the small side but the location is fantastic; and I know your job is a bit crap but your social life is terrific. I'm telling you, Rach, moving to Barcelona was the best thing that you have ever done. Gone are the days where you worked unsocial hours, received a billion emails a day and had to put up with Vicky Big Bum bossing you around. Now you're planning a new exciting career, have time to write letters to your nearest and dearest and have a bronzed muscular boyfriend! Boy, do I need to find myself a DIY expert if they are all as buff as him! Seriously, though, darl, I think Bertie is wonderful; he's funny, smart and the way he looks at you is just sickening! Lol

I also really liked Lucy. At first I have to say I was really nervous about meeting my 'replacement' and was hoping she'd be horrible so I could bitch about her to Rory but she wasn't at all and again, I'm really pleased you're making nice friends. Next time, however, I'm coming back in summer and we are hitting the beach. It is so depressing here, Rach; the weather forecast is predicting snow and spring is nowhere to be seen. Yesterday I posed for my Postage Pinup shoot and it's just as well I was holding up a pair of beach balls in front of my chest, as it was rather nippy to say the least! The photos looked great, though, and Andy, the photographer, said I was a natural.

This weekend I am doing nothing. I'm planning on staying inside, wearing my onesie and watching back-to-back episodes of 'Sex and the City' whilst doing my nails, eating junk food and generally being a lazy fat cow. What are you up to?

Love you,

Suz xx

8th March

Dear Mrs. Ashley (Gill),

I hope you don't mind me getting your address off Mum but I wanted to write to send my love and say how I'm thinking of you during this difficult time. She tells me that you're doing well at the moment and in fighting spirits, which is great. I was telling her about how you were the best teacher I've ever had. Truly inspirational and kind and always willing to listen no matter how insignificant the problem seemed to be.

My time in your lessons wasn't wasted either, you'll be pleased to hear, as finally, after far too long working as a hotel receptionist, I've decided to set up my own business. You showed me how to make my first cupcakes and it just so happens that I'm now thinking of starting up my own café, making them for a living. My years of Uni studying Travel and Tourism led me into the world of Hotel Management but, to tell the truth, I never thought I'd be standing behind a reception desk for so long. So instead of another 10 years giving fake smiles and hotel room keys I'm going to set up my own tearoom here in Barcelona. Perhaps once you've beaten this thing you'd like to come over with Mr. Ashley (Tom) and sample my cakes and see if they are up to the standard of the amazing butterfly cakes you used to make.

I'm off down the beach now to shoot my photo for the Postage Pinups Project. Mum apparently thinks it's 30 degrees all year round - little does she know that in March it's actually bloody cold and I'm going to be on the beach in nothing but a smile and a carefully positioned Spanish fan! Can't wait to see the rest of the pictures!

All my love,

Rachel xxx

10th March

Dearest Rachel,

I'm sorry, but today I can only spare time for a short letter. Tomorrow I'm having my photo taken for the Pinup Project and I need to spend at least a couple of hours at the gym on the cross trainer as I'm a little bit worried that the Christmas present I'm holding up to hide my saggy bits really needs to be twice the size it actually is. I also need to put up the fake Christmas Tree and decorate the fireplace at the Manor so it's ready for the shoot tomorrow.

Normally, I'm much more on top of things but Robert has been keeping me so busy. Dinners here, outings there, romantic liaisons booked - oh, it's been dreamy, don't get me wrong - but my usual routines have been neglected and I'm just feeling a little bit stressed. It doesn't help that I'm on a strict diet to lose weight and I'm reduced to eat crummy old salads while he tucks into a steak, oblivious to my cause. It's been such a long time since I was courted in this way and I think I just need a little space. My independence is so important to me and really don't want to lose it. I have to say our Easter escape can't come too soon.

Will let you know how the shoot goes in my next letter. Your Mum is having her photo taken as we speak. Andy is a real darling but he's also a perfectionist. Something that's important to all of us but when you're outside in 6 inches of snow hiding behind a snowman with no top on, I think you'd settle for almost perfect. Must dash; I've just been instructed to fill a hot water bottle, as your mother is turning blue!

Much love,

Miss Elaine x

P.S: I now know where you get your ample cleavage from!

12th March

Dear Gemma,

I'm so glad that you seemed happier in your last letter. It's bloody hard work trying to stay positive when you're stuck in a crap job; God knows I suffer but you just can't let them win. This week Madam Sanchez has been unbearable. Nothing has been good enough and everyone has had to walk around on eggshells so we don't set her off. On the plus side, though, Lucy and I have put together a business plan for our Typical English Tearoom and one of the girls in my language exchange class, Maria, has helped me translate it into Spanish and Catalan (I would move to a part of the world that has two languages to learn!!) so that we can present it to the bank next week. We've booked a meeting to see if we can get a loan to go alongside the money we're investing and also the support from Miss Elaine. Fingers crossed they will accept it and then we can start looking for a suitable place to rent. It's all coming together so quickly but I don't want to get too excited as we don't officially have the funds yet.

How did the job hunting go? See anything you liked the look of? I always thought you'd be good working

229

outdoors. When you were living in Wales you were always outside going for walks or tending to your garden. Perhaps you could do something linked to that?

By the way my friend Suz wants to come visit over the summer too; I think you guys met at my leaving do, so how about I send you her details and perhaps between the two of you, if you'd be happy with that, plan flights etc and I'll book you in. We could spend some time here in Barcelona then maybe a few days up the coast on the Costa Brava. While you're here you'll defo have to join us for one of Alberto's paellas, oh my goodness they're amazing! His mother taught him how to cook it (something I think all good Spanish mothers teach their children) and it's just packed with delicious seafood and flavours. Mind you I do always pick out the octopus tentacles as they freak me out.

Lots of love,

Rachel x

15th March

Dear Suz,

Happy Birthday, honey! Wishing you an amazing day and wish I could be there to celebrate. Please find enclosed a small but gorgeous birthday gift - but don't open it before the special day. Rory phoned me the other day and told me the gays are taking you out for dinner in Brighton. He said that after your 'onesie weekend' last week you needed to dress up and get out for a boogie. I wholeheartedly support him in this proposal and suggest you also go to that lovely cocktail bar in the South Lanes. I intend to take Alberto there one day, as it would be great to show him all my favourite places in the UK.

Things are going really well at the moment. We see each other about three or four times a week and just get on so well. Now that my Spanish is slowly improving, I'm also attempting the odd phrase with him - but I still make so many mistakes, including a major humiliating one the other day, when I ordered a roast chicken from a local shop - only to make the fatal mistake of asking for a 'polla' instead of a 'pollo'. Only one letter difference yet one is a chicken and the other is a cock!!! The man behind the counter then laughed and said something, which sounded filthy and I went bright red and left with my 'pollo' tucked under my arm!

My next Spanish exam is coming up next week yet I'm not too hopeful of passing. I've spent so much time on planning and preparing for our meeting with the bank concerning our business plan that all my studying has gone out the window. Still, it's about prioritizing and we needed to get it done. I'm really nervous though, Suz, as I'm kind of pinning all hopes on this. I really don't want to stay forever under Madam Sanchez's beck and call but equally, I get scared that without my current position I wouldn't be able to do any other job as my Spanish isn't good enough. Thankfully for me it turns out Lucy is a bit of a language expert and despite her starting in my Spanish class, seems to have recalled all her A level Spanish skills and is now at Grade 4 level, which means she can deal with all the bits of the business that involve translation and paper work and I can concentrate on the cooking and decoration. Wish me luck honey.

Happy Birthday once more and remember this piece of advice you've told me many a time in the past; growing old is mandatory but growing up is optional!

Have fun,

Rach xxx

17th March

Dear Rachel,

Well, my dear, the ladies have all done their part now so it's down to the men to do theirs. All the photos are in the can as they say and I have to admit they are looking super. How dare that Madam Sanchez say you've put on weight? Your picture was wonderful, darling. I especially like the waves splashing in the background. How did you get it without anyone else on the beach, I thought it would be full of sunbathers. We aren't all as lucky as you, my dear, with the weather and I literally froze my tits off taking my shot but it was worth it. Your father says it's his favourite one - mind you he couldn't really say anything else and Andy said I was a natural!

All the pictures have now been passed on to an old friend of your father's who works in the printing trade. He's kindly arranged for us to have all the cards made up for free on recycled card as long as we mention his company in the articles, which we naturally will. The whole printing process takes a while, though, so we won't get to see the final results for about 6 weeks. That's still in plenty of time, though, before the Summer Fair that Lord Robert is going to organize at Latchington Manor with the aim of getting as many people to support the charity as possible. It would be super if you were able to come darling. As soon as I know more I'll let you know.

However one has suffered for my art and after spending an hour out in the snow, (which has now, thankfully, gone), I've ended up full of cold and feeling really rather crappy. I'm currently writing to you from my bed, which is surrounded by tissues, a hot steaming Lemsip and a jar of Vicks VapoRub, which your father seems to enjoy rubbing in my chest a little too much! Having said that, he's been a very good boy and has been looking after me very well. He's collected my prescription from the doctor, prepared my meals and even set up the portable TV in the corner of the room so I don't need to leave my bed. I daren't go into the kitchen to see the mess he's no doubt made but I guess I can deal with that once I'm up out of bed again.

Hopefully, now I have some tablets from the doctor, I'll start improving. I couldn't stand another week in bed, as I'd possibly die of boredom. Daytime TV really is terrible; if I see those awful Loose Women one more time I'll scream - and as for the horrendous things they do to people's houses on 60 Minute Make Over, it's enough to make you weep. I've mostly been reading; however, I'm now on my last book so will need to stock up at the library next week. I've just finished reading Fifty Shades of Grey. One of the ladies at the hairdressers recommended it to me. Well, at first I thought what kind of person did she think I was but after a few chapters I was hooked. You really should give it a go, darling; I'm definitely going to read the next two. I wonder if they have them in the village library? Anyway, I'm going to have a sleep now, all these drugs are knocking me out and the doctor says sleeping is good for me.

Love, peace and happiness,

Mum and Dad xxx

P.S: Please find enclosed six recipes for cakes which I think would go down extremely well in your future café. They are quite old fashioned but I think if you're going for a typically English Teashop then you really should try them out.

P.P.S: If this letter doesn't get to you it's because I gave it to your father to post, as I can't leave the house and he's probably not put enough stamps on the envelope.

19th March,

Dear Rachel,

Thank you so much for your letter. It was so kind of you to write and even kinder of you to strip off naked in March, on the beach, and have your photo taken for the Pinup Project.

I'm feeling ok at the moment but the chemo really takes it out of you. Everyone is being so kind and helpful, though, and Tom has just been the perfect support. I thought I just had a stomach bug or was suffering from IBS at the time. When the doctor told me it was cancer, I was rather taken aback and that's why I never told anyone. I really didn't want to fuss but when I see what good everyone is doing and what a difference we might make for myself and others, I'm happy that Tom told your mother. She's been such a support and I do understand that standing back and seeing someone you love suffer can make you feel useless, so this is a jolly good way for everyone to feel like they are fighting it with me.

I was so happy to hear about your business idea and would love to come and see you once I'm fully recovered. Hopefully I will get some good news in the next month or so. You always were talented in the kitchen. I think I only had to explain to you what to do once and, thereafter, you relied on your natural baking skills, and even showed the rest of the class what to do. I know teachers aren't meant to have favourites but you really were mine!

If there's one thing I've learnt from this, Rachel, it's that you need to live your life and not waste a moment on things that aren't making you happy. I'm very much looking forward to seeing the Pinup cards in their final glory. I understand there's going to be a charity fate at Latchington Manor in early June; it would be lovely to see you there if you can make it.

Thank you once again for your kind words,

Gill xxx

P.S: There's no need to call me Mrs. Ashley anymore!

20th March

Dear Rach,

I've been in touch with Suz and we're coming in the last week in July for a week in the sun. I so need it as school has, once again, descended into madness and my positivity has slowly been chipped away by arseholes! The chief arsehole is the Minister for Education, who has never been near a state school in his life, let alone taught at one; then arseholes number two are Ofsted, who inspect the schools that they know nothing about and then finally, our Head Teacher, Mrs. Hoxton, who sits in her office all day pretending to look busy when in fact she's playing Candy Crush on her iPhone!

As you can tell, I'm a little stressed as we had the Ofsted call to arms last week and after a three day inspection, we were left to pick up the pieces. I wouldn't mind, Rach, if they were there to support us and if they actually knew what we do on a 'day-to-day' basis but they don't. They come in and all they're interested in is levels and data. They don't seem to even care about the children, about the individuals or all the creative things that go on in schools.

I got observed during an English class and instead of asking the children what they were writing about, the inspector went around asking what level they thought they were and if they knew how to make it better. What kind of message does that send to children? Anyway, it confirmed my decision to leave and last night I sent my CV off to a National Trust property to work as their education officer. I thought it looked perfect, linked to teaching and working with children but away from all the endless crap linked to state education these days. Anyway will wait and see. If that fails then perhaps I'll run away and join the circus!

It makes me feel really cross, though, as I love working with the kids and even though some are challenging, we always end up having fun, and seeing them learn and create is just brilliant. I'm just so tired of feeling like I'm failing all the time. Oh dear, I feel like the emergency chocolate/wine cupboard might need to be raided once more!

Take care, honey, and thanks for listening to all my moans,

Gemma xx

24th March

Dear Rachel,

My birthday weekend was terrific. I wish you could have been there - however, you were with us in spirit; mainly vodka! The boys took me to a fabulous Chinese restaurant where we stuffed ourselves with all sorts of yummy delights. I started well enough with the chopsticks but after a few glasses of vino had to resort to a fork. I'm terribly jealous of you and Rory you know. His boyfriend, Harry, is also a right dish and wonderfully funny. I can only hope to find someone as nice as the guys you've both found. Anyway, enough of the boyfriend envy, the rest of the night was also great as we had cocktails in Browns and then went dancing in a club on the seafront where I was surrounded by hot men all night - and every single one of them was gay; highly frustrating but plenty of fun.

Then on Sunday, I recovered with an amazing Sunday roast - something that would make you jealous - and unwrapped all my lovely gifts. The necklace you got me, honey, was indeed gorgeous and I'm wearing it right now. I'll have to choose something equally as stunning for your birthday in a few months time.

Your friend, Gemma, got in touch and we've decided to come to visit at the end of July. By my calculations, the sea will be a nice temperature by then and I will hopefully have lost a stone if I stay off the ice-cream. We seriously need to get Gemma laid, though, as she is one stressed teacher. I suggest we get her tipsy, get Alberto to introduce her to a nice Spanish boy and then let the rest work itself out! I mean work is work but you've got to know when to switch off from it. I've invited her out for drinks next weekend in the aim of warming her up for the summer hols. Give me a few weeks with her and I'll sort her out.

Lots of love, darl,

Suz x

25th March

Dear Mum and Dad,

I had some amazing news yesterday. Lucy and I went to the bank and to cut a long story short, they are going to give us the money!!! I'm so happy, Mum, this is the start of something wonderful, I just know it. So next we have to find a suitable space to rent and set up shop. It's not going to be easy but dreams don't work unless you do! And that's exactly what we intend to do. Unfortunately, I'll need to keep working at the hotel a little longer but the end will soon be in sight and I'll be able to wave Madam Sanchez goodbye.

How are you feeling now? I hope the Lemsips have kicked in and you've not been subjected to any more episodes of Loose Women. If you think daytime TV is bad in the UK you should be glad you've not got Spanish TV! Glad Dad's been looking after you, I always remember whenever I got ill he'd always be there to take care of me.

Thanks for the recipes, by the way. I actually had a baking day this week and made three of the cakes. The classic Victoria Sponge was a great success and was given to Belen to share with all her friends from aqua aerobics. The coffee cake was easy and came up a treat. I changed the icing for water icing, however, as the butter icing was a bit sickly. That was passed on to Alberto and all his friends. He loves coffee so I'm sure I'll be baking variations on that one. The final chocolate cake however was a bit of a disaster. It tasted delicious, the texture was perfect but it ended up looking like a massive cowpat! You see, I decided to bake it in a new rose shaped silicon mould I bought recently; the reality was rather different, though, as instead of coming out looking like a beautiful rose, it more closely resembled a huge turd! I actually roared with laughter as it came out and couldn't stop. At first I thought I'd have to throw it away but instead, covered it in chocolate then added summer berries by the ton to disguise it and in the end it actually looked rather special and not at all like a cowpat. I ended up taking it into work and sharing it out. Madam Sanchez even took a slice and instead of the usual insults said it was delicious! Miracles do happen!

Lots of love,

Rachel xxx

P.S: I've booked my flights for the week of the Summer Fair in July and good news! Alberto is coming too. I thought it was time for him to see where I grew up and seeing as the whole Village will be attending the fair it's also a good opportunity to show him off to everyone!

P.P.S: No, I've not read Fifty Shades of Grey and I'm not sure I like it that my mother is! Are you sure those drugs the doctor gave you didn't go to your head? I'd stick to your usual books if I were you, Mum!

29th March

Dearest Rachel,

I'm so glad you got the funding you needed from the bank. That is exciting news indeed. I was only too happy to support you with my share also and am looking forward to seeing your ideas when I visit next month. As I said before, I am more than happy to be a silent partner but one thing I do insist on and that is that you bake me one of your lemon drizzle cakes when I'm over. The one at your leaving party was just divine and the Waitrose one just doesn't match up.

Talking of Waitrose, I witnessed a very funny scene in there two days ago. I was minding my own business, choosing a bottle of wine to have with dinner, when all this commotion broke out in the aisle opposite. I naturally poked my nose round the corner to see what was going on and saw two women on the floor covered in water. I carefully tiptoed through the puddle to help and saw it was Pauline, the Vicars wife, alongside one of the Waitrose cleaners. It was all rather confusing at first and both ladies were rather angry with one another; it was only when Pauline started to explain what had happened that it all started to make sense.

You see, Pauline's eyesight is rather poor - that's why she always sits in the front row for any of the Am Dram productions - and as she was going round the shop she felt someone try to take her basket from her. She reacted by pulling it back and swinging it at the thief but then found herself and the thief falling to the floor whilst being covered in water. You see what Pauline didn't realize was that, due to her bad eyesight, after popping her basket down to look at the price of Baked Beans she accidentally picked up the cleaners bucket of water instead. Then the cleaner came looking for her bucket and tried to take it from Pauline, who thought it was a bag snatcher, hence the two of them ending up on the floor covered in water.

Once Pauline realized what she had done she was ever so apologetic and said she'd book an appointment with the optician as soon as possible. The cleaner gave a bit of a grunt, picked up her bucket and muttered something about having to bloody clean up another aisle now. I stayed impartial and made sure Pauline saw her way out through the doors correctly and went back to my wines. Who needs television when you have all that on your doorstep!

By the way, darling, I meant to apologize, for my previous letter. I was feeling ever so stressed that day and let it out in that letter. Thankfully the photo shoot was a success and Andy said I was a natural model. With that taken care of, I then realized my mood must have been related to the month of dieting and fitness I put myself through and have sworn not to do anything so daft again. Robert and I are once again on very good terms and we're heading to the New Forest for the weekend. It's apparently a spa hotel but he's guaranteed me it's not a health one where you can only eat lentils the entire time you're there. If that turns out not to be the case I'll be escaping and heading off down the local pub for bangers and mash!

Love and hugs,

Miss Elaine x

Chapter 9
April – George And The Dragon

1st April

Dear Rach,

How are things going? I hear congratulations are in order for your new business! And now you have the money, it's time for the exciting bits; finding the space, buying the soft furnishings and deciding which magazines you'll have on the counter. If I were you, I'd use fresh cut flowers on each table and pop to IKEA to pick out all their lovely bits and bobs from the cutlery to the tablecloths. If you want any advice from two homos with impeccable taste, you know where we are.

I've also got some exciting news, as Harry has asked me to move in with him! It's only been three months - which kind of freaked me out a bit - but after taking a bit of time to think about it, I said 'yes'. It's a little bit crazy but we get on so well and it would also save us both driving back and forth to see each other constantly. I'm also ready to move out of the village; it's been a wonderful home but I so need a change and I love being by the seaside. Waking up next to my beautiful man, then taking the dogs for a walk on the seafront is just the perfect way to start a day. I'm going to move at the end of the month. That will give me time to serve notice on my flat and to pack everything up. I'm nervous but excited at the same time. I feel like an adult for the first time!

When you're over in the summer, you'll have to come down and see the place; it's not far from that fabulous ice-cream shop on Hove seafront.

The only downside is the bloody seagulls, however. They wake you up in the morning from their screeching, they shit on your car when it's parked out the front and then they dive bomb you if you have food in your hand. The other day one even landed on my shoulder as I was about to tuck into a sausage roll from the local bakery and the bastard flew off with the entire thing in its mouth! Serves me right for eating fatty old sausage rolls, I guess. Do you get seagulls in Barcelona? I remember seeing those bright green screeching parrots but no seagulls.

So when are you telling Madam Sanchez you're quitting? Would love to see the look on her face when you tell her. Mind you prepare yourself for a final month of hell no doubt. I once took great glee in telling an employer to shove his job - and then for the final month had to do all the crappy jobs that no one else wanted to do. I don't regret it, though, as it was such a great feeling; mind you I was only 18 and it's probably not worth making enemies when you're setting up a new business as you never know who knows who out there.

Got to go - off to bingo night. It's not as bad as it sounds, it's actually a real hoot as the caller is a drag queen named Miss. Dolly Mixture and all the number combinations are a little bit rude! Right up your street I'd say!

Love,

Rory and Mr. Paws x

P.S: Mr. Paws sends his love. He's currently trying to sniff his own butt but I know deep down that he's really sending a message of love to you. It's just his way of showing it!

3rd April

Dear Sus,

Lucy and I spent the whole weekend looking round spaces to convert into our café and found nothing suitable. We saw ten different places and each had major faults: too small, too far out of the city, too much work needed doing, nice area but no outside area, bad area but lovely space, no light, too much light... The list goes on. It was, however, our first round of searching so hopefully things can only get better. We'll see another few in the evenings this week and then the agent said they'd find us some more for the following weekend too. I can picture so clearly in my mind's eye how it will look but I guess I just have to match that up with the places that are available to us on our budget.

As a break from work and new business stuff, Alberto took me to a fabulous little Chinese dumpling restaurant in El Borne called 'Mosquito'. It's the part of the city with all the lovely posh independent-style clothes shop, where you bought those gorgeous red shoes that you said you just had to have - even though you'd have to eat nothing but beans on toast for a month so you could afford them. The food was just heavenly. There are not so many good Chinese restaurants in Barcelona but this one is a gem and I will be returning very soon. It also had these beautiful fabric lanterns that I'm adding to my notebook of café style ideas. Everywhere I go now I'm taking photos or noting down ideas so I can be inspired for when we get to decorate our place.

How are things with you? Mum said you were a little down last time she saw you. Give me a buzz if you need a friend to talk to.

Love,

Rachel xxx

3rd April

Dear Rachel,

I'm glad you liked the cake recipes I sent. I would have loved to have seen the cowpat cake, sounds hilarious! I remember once making a no-flour chocolate cake and getting confused with the recipe and ended up putting far too much mixture into the cake tin. After returning to the oven 45 minutes later, it had doubled in size and was running out of the gaps in the oven! It looked like the time Bertie (our dog Bertie, not yours) got the 'yuk yuks' and exploded all over the neighbours' driveway! Took me all bloody morning to clean it up too!

You'll be glad to hear I'm now fully recovered and back on my feet again. Apparently, the bug went round most of the village but thankfully all your father's TLC worked wonders and now I'm back to my normal self. Being out of routine for almost two weeks, though, means I have to do lots of catching up on things, so this week your father and I need to do a big food shop, do the garden and visit Great Aunt Shelly, who, I fear, is starting to lose it. I called her to arrange popping round and she thought I was her sister, Betty, who died ten years ago. She then recognized me but it's not the first time she's had an episode like that. It worries me as she's on her own but I dread even mentioning a 'home' to her. Well let's see, perhaps when we go round she'll be fine; after all, voices on a telephone can sound very similar.

One thing I did manage to do this week, however, was pop into the local library to hand back a few books and see if they had a

Miss. Marple - yes I'm still thinking about auditioning later in the year - and the next Fifty Shades of Grey, only to find that the main check-out desk had disappeared and had been replaced by three machines. Now, as you know, I'm absolutely hopeless with any kind of technology - it takes me twenty minutes to work out which of those remote thingies to use to change the TV channel - and although I was never fond of the stern-looking woman who used to stamp the books, I didn't want her to be replaced by a machine. What is the world coming to? Everyone seems determined to go all James-Bond-gadgets on us though and now the Library has joined them! I'm sure that one of these days we'll be taken over by robots!

Anyway, I found a couple of Marple's and a Maeve Binchy (there's a 3 month waiting list for the Fifty Shades Books!) and proceeded to the machines. Well, two of them were not functioning; good start! The other had a queue of five people. So when it came to my turn, I didn't know what to do with it. I tried scanning the book like they do in Waitrose and that made it beep but then didn't know if I had taken the books back or renewed them. The man behind me started to tut impatiently so I asked if he wanted to go ahead but he said I needed to finish first. Then after a further five minutes of pushing buttons and scanning my library card, the machine obviously gave up hope and also reported that it wasn't functioning! The man behind me tutted some more so I gave him an evil stare and went to find someone to help. I reasoned a human must still stack the shelves - unless robots also did that these days. I then found the stern-looking librarian in the Gardening section and explained to her what had happened. She also tutted at me and took me to a new counter, round to the side, where she stamped the books manually and took back the old ones. I then gave her my library card and she explained to me that the reason the machine wasn't working was because I was trying to get books out on my bus pass! Well, I wasn't to know; they all look the same to me these days! Next time I think I'll ask Suz to come with me to work it out so I don't get tutted at again!

Love, peace and happiness,

Mum and Dad xxx

P.S: Your father and I have booked our flights to Barcelona and made reservations at that hotel you suggested for mid-June. Can't wait to see my little girl and meet Alberto!

8th April

Dear Miss Elaine,

No need to apologize at all. I know how stressful life can get and I certainly know what it's like starting a new relationship. I really think the problem is Men in General. Now, I'm not saying our guys are typical men as we both seem to have found a great pair of the male species but even they have their little ways, don't they?

For example I can honestly say I am falling head over heels in love with Alberto but I don't love the way he gets in from work and leaves his sweaty clothes piled on the floor. Neither am I enamoured of the way he cuts his toenails in the lounge and lets the nail clippings fly all over the place. However, it is still early days and I know compromises are needed, especially when I think about my own faults, which are possibly endless! So don't worry, Miss Elaine, your worries are the same as mine and no doubt those of every other women out there in the world too!

As for the dieting and exercise, I'm afraid I'm not the one to ask for advice. Every time I'm 'good' and go to the gym or lose a little weight, I then reward myself with a massive cake or something equally naughty, which kind of ruins the whole point of being 'good' in the first place. It doesn't help living in a country that is obsessed with bread. It's everywhere and I just can't seem to say no. However Alberto seems to like the way I look so perhaps we should stop beating ourselves up over it and just be content with our muffin tops and bingo wings.

Looking forward to having you visit. I've arranged a surprise for you one night that I know you'll just love so try to fit something glamorous (as if you wouldn't be packing everything glamorous anyway!) into your suitcase as we're going to be going somewhere posh for an evening. I'm not saying anything more but let's just say it will bring out your dramatic side!

Lots of love,

Rachel x

P.S How is the Vicar's wife? Has she been to Spec Savers yet?!

10th April

Dear Mum and Dad,

Been to the library this week? You do make me laugh. Your skills with technology make me look like an IT genius! I do agree, though; I sometimes wish I had been born in the times of Elizabeth Bennet and Mr. Darcy where texting, tweeting and emailing were non-existent and "social media" meant actually going out to meet people. With my luck, though, I'd probably end up being a scullery maid instead of a Lady and my life would be totally unglamourous, stuck in a kitchen and smelling of bleach or some sort of soap powder.

I'm so glad you guys have sorted out your flights at last. It will be lovely to show you round and for you to see my little 'el flato'. I've told Belen and she can't wait to meet you. I've been teaching her a few words to say to you in English. The rest I might have to translate if I know what she's going on about. I still find it very frustrating at times and sometimes I just feel so stupid. The other day we went out to a birthday party and whilst Alberto was talking to someone I was chatting, in English, to a really nice lady who runs a tea shop in the city. Then while we were chatting a guy came up and started speaking in Spanish, I naturally responded best I could in Spanish but after a while found it too hard and just stood and listened. Then later in the evening I continued talking in English again with Monica (The tea woman who might supply us with tea!) and he told me I needed to try harder, and how typically English I was. I got really upset and told him how difficult it was when there were lots of people talking at once and with music playing as well but he didn't care. That's when Alberto came over and saved me and told the guy to back off. I felt bad that I wasn't better at speaking Spanish but at the same time felt angry that a stranger would speak to me that way and not understand how challenging it can be. Still, it's made me more determined to learn and I know I'll get better; I just need to do a little at a time.

Miss Elaine arrives early next week for our Easter getaway to Madrid. She arrives on the 16th and stays for a couple of days in Barcelona and then we head down to Madrid on the AVE high speed train. Very exciting! Will send you a postcard from the city. It's also the same time that Victoria Plum arrives in Barcelona; I've not told her yet that I'm not going to be here. Naughty, I know, but I just couldn't bear to see her again and especially not when I'd have to be waiting on her at the hotel. Instead, I've asked Eva, the other receptionist, to pass on a note to her for me with a complementary bottle of cava by way of an apology.

Love,

Rachel xxx

12th April

Dear Rachel,

You'll never guess what, dear, but your father has just won us two tickets on a cruise! We've never won anything before, except if you count the time your father's marrow came first in the Village Fair a couple of years back. The letter about the cruise came quite out of the blue really and now I'm in a bit of a panic as it's only in a week's time! You see, he entered a photography competition months ago to win a Luxury Cruise for two people round the British Isles. To enter you needed to send in a photo of something traditionally British so he sent in a wonderful picture of you and Miss Elaine from the pantomine. It was just as you were preparing to go to the ball and Miss Elaine was waving her wand around. I helped him pick the photo out, naturally; after all, what's more British than a good old pantomime? Well, he only went and won it - but the notification letter got lost in the bloody post and we only received it yesterday! We phoned up immediately and just as well we did, as they were about to contact the 2nd prizewinner and give it to them. I asked why hadn't they phoned and they told me your father hadn't put a telephone number on the entry form. Well, if he hadn't just won us a cruise I would have bollocked him! However, we are going on a Luxury Criuse, leaving from Southampton next week for 10 days and I'm beyond excited!

We've never been on a cruise before so not really sure what to expect but I know they are usually rather smart affairs. I've cleared our schedule for the next week and your father and I are going clothes shopping - something he hates, but it needs to be done. Can't be seen on a Luxury Cruise in our normal weekday clothes. They are sending us our tickets and a guide to the cruise in the post this week, so fingers crossed this one doesn't get lost in the post!

Must go as I only have a week to get all the ironing done, packing sorted and your father organized!

Love, peace and Luxury Cruises!

Mum and Dad xxx

15th April

Hey darl,
I'm fine - just feeling a little low at the moment. I've been wanting to call you but know how busy you've been with your new business etc., so kind of didn't, which was stupid because you could have snapped me out of this feeling much quicker than I'm snapping myself out of it.

It's just that I look around me and see how much you guys are all moving on with your lives and getting boyfriends - and I'm kind of not. You've got your new business, a new friend to set it up with and a gorgeous boyfriend..... It's not that I'm jealous, though, because I'm so happy for you, darling, it's just I that want the same. Rory is moving away and I know it's not far but he'll be all cozy with Harry and what about me? I can't keep dating these boys for the rest of my life, even if they do have amazing bodies. I want something special too, even your friend Gemma, who I criticised, is doing something about her life. Did she get that job, by the way?

I know I have a good job but I don't take it seriously; in fact I don't take life that seriously. Is that a problem? Maybe I should go back home to Oz and find a new life there. At least there I'd be near my folks and could see my nephews and nieces grow up. Either that or I just need a slap round the mush and told to get a grip on things.

Sorry not to tell you this over the phone, honey, but actually, in a strange way, it feels better to have written it down. Who would have thought your annoying letter writing project would have converted me into a writer!

Love you,

Suz xx

18th April

Dear Victoria,

I'm so sorry I wasn't able to see you during your visit to Barcelona but I've been whisked away to Madrid for important business and won't be back until next week. Please accept this bottle of cava on my behalf. Enjoy your stay and feel free to contact Madam Sanchez if things are not up to your high standards.

Kind regards,

Rachel

24th April

Dear Rachel,

Kevin and I were terribly disappointed not to have seen you whilst we were in Barcelona. The trip just wasn't the same. Madam Sanchez was a delightful woman, though, and we were both impressed with the way she ran the hotel. The cava you left us was most pleasant but we both commented how it wasn't cold.

How was your trip to Madrid? I didn't even realise you had an Aunt in Peru. I told Madam Sanchez that you had never even mentioned her to me and that as far as I was concerned you only had a Great Aunt Shelly.

Since returning to the UK I'm sad to report that both Kevin and I have had the most terrible diarrhoea. The local pharmacist said it was probably a bug we picked up on the aeroplane but I'm convinced it was the local food - why we even tried it I'm not sure. We're both now on a diet of plain white rice and crackers.

Will we be seeing you at the Summer Fair in July? I hear there's some sort of launch event going on. I've not got to the bottom of it yet but when I do I'll let you know.

Kind regards,

Victoria

24th April

Dear Suz,

Well, you old cow, I hope my phone call last night
sorted you right out. I'm following up said phone
call with one of my 'annoying' letters so you really
take note of what I said. You my lovely are one of
the brightest, most passionate and positive people I
know. Your outlook on life is so wonderful, Suz, it's
not just a matter of treating life seriously or not,
you treat life as something to live and you do it really
rather well. And yes, you do have a good job and you
are good at it but that's not to say you can't strive
for more. You know how that place runs better than
any of them. Go in there and show them that you
deserve more. Then if they don't value you the way
you feel you should be valued, look for something
else.

As for the love life, there's no answer to that one.
I've learnt that things happen when they happen, there
are no rules, there is no secret formula, you just
have to be yourself and it's often a case of being at
the right place at the right time.

Finally, as I said yesterday, Rory and I are not going

anywhere. Yes, we're a little further away than we once were but that doesn't mean we care about you any the less or that you can't visit whenever you like. However, I have a sneaking suspicion that Alberto is taking me away for a romantic weekend for my birthday so you need to stay away that particular weekend! LOL

Now, I'm expecting one of your sickening animal cards in one week's time and unless it's filled with all sorts of positive stuff, I'm booking the next flight out there to see you and sort you out. Either that or I'll pass your address on to Vicky Big Bum who will hound you until you die a lonely crazy cat woman!

Love you loads, you silly moo cow!

Rachel xxx

P.S: Would you believe it? Mum and Dad won a Luxury Cruise holiday round the British Isles! Dad entered a competition for 'A Great British Photo' and used one of Miss Elaine and me in the pantomime. Since I was the subject of the photo I did feel like asking where my prize was....... but, never mind, they deserve it.

April 25th

Dear Mum and Dad,

How was the cruise? I still can't believe you won something that good. Tell Dad to buy a lottery ticket too. You never know, he might be on a lucky streak! Looking forward to hearing all about it.

Miss Elaine and I have just returned from Madrid and had such a fun-filled time. Perhaps Dad should enter more competitions and you'll win a holiday there too! Before we went to Madrid, however, we had a couple of days in Barcelona and it just so happened that Miss Elaine was with Lucy and me when we found the perfect location for the café. We were wandering round the city on my own guided tour (I'll do the same for you when you visit) when we spotted a place in a very popular street in Sant Antoni, not far from my flat. Miss Elaine insisted we call the number of the letting agents who said their office was actually very close and that if we wanted to we could see it. Twenty minutes later the agent appeared and we went inside. It was just meant to be, Mum, it was the perfect size, nice and light; there was a little kitchen and space outside for a few tables if we got a terrace licence. The agent asked if we needed time to think about it but all three of us were convinced: we signed on the dotted line there and then!

We'll need to do a little work on it but as it used to be a bar, it's actually pretty much set up for us. Next week we just need to complete the paper work and then the keys will be ours! I'm so happy and it was just super that Miss Elaine could be there to see it with us.

That evening I took Miss Elaine to the Opera at the Liceu Theatre. It was my first time there, too, and my first Opera so it was doubly exciting! The theatre itself is spectacular and we both dressed up in our finest clothes. I did invite Alberto but he said it wasn't his cup of tea. Miss Elaine and I both thoroughly enjoyed it, however, and managed to follow what was going on even though it was in Italian. It was all so flamboyant and passionate and the venue just added to the sheer elegance of it all. It was also nice to go somewhere where you weren't forced to listen to people shovelling popcorn into their mouths and suck on over-priced and over-sized cokes.

The following day we then travelled to Madrid on the

wonderful high speed train and after a few hours of gossiping found ourselves in the centre of the city. The train station on arrival was certainly a pretty impressive start to our trip as it was a huge glass covered arboretum full of plants and palm trees. The rest of the city didn't disappoint either and for the next few days we enjoyed touring the city and taking in all the wonderful art and architecture.

Our hotel was wonderful; Miss Elaine certainly knows how to pick a good one and insisted on paying as I had put her up in Barcelona. Hardly the equivalent, I told her, but she said she was happy to do it. We had a few gorgeous meals out and we found the chocolate and churros café, too, that everyone had been telling me to visit. All in all, it was a wonderful break. Miss Elaine then flew out from Madrid and I went back to Barcelona on the train.

Then upon returning I quit my job, which gave me immense satisfaction. Madam Sanchez was none too pleased, especially as she worked out that my trip away with my "Aunt from Peru" wasn't entirely true – but there was nothing she could do about it.

The next month is going to be tough working full time

at the hotel as well as making lots of decisions for the café but it's going to be so worth it.

Lots of love,

Rachel xxx

P.S: Keep an eye on Suz for me, Mum. She's been feeling a bit down recently and just needs looking after.

27th April

Dear Gemma,

I got the loan from the bank, I quit my job and we found a space for the café! My goodness the past month has been life changing. According to Madam Sanchez, there are already too many coffee shops in Barcelona and we won't make a profit - but there's no way I'm listening to that negative old cow. She's put me on shift work for the last month I'm at the hotel; she says it's because of hotel procedures when there's a change over between staff but I know it's just her way of punishing me. However what she doesn't realise is that now that I'm doing 3 late shifts a week (10pm to 5am!), I'm not really bothered by her or any of the customers, as they are all in bed or coming home from nights out, which means I have time to surf the net and plan out the café how I want it.

I've only done my first three night shifts so not had time to do much but so far have visited the websites of other cafes to check them out and I've become a Pinterest fiend. I absolutely love it. There are so many ideas on there, especially for decoration but also for cake recipes and smoothies. Can't wait until next week's night shifts, actually!

I know you are a book fan, Gem; well you'd love the way they celebrate Saint Georges Day out here. Here, in Catalonia, he's known as Sant Jordi but basically he's the same Saint George who slew the dragon and saved the princess. Turns out loads of countries actually have him for their patron saint as well as England, only here they actually celebrate the day in style. Schools and neighbourhoods all retell the story and act out the play whilst the day itself has been linked in with World Book Day, so there are bookstalls all over the city. It's also considered a day of romance (even more so than Saint Valentine's) and traditionally the women receive a red rose and the men get a book. Luckily for me, however, Alberto isn't too traditional and as he knows how much I like reading bought me a book and a rose.

He bought me 'Shadows Of The Wind' by Carlos Ruiz Zafon; it's apparently all about Barcelona in the civil war, as well as being an exciting love story. Can't wait to read it. What are you reading at the moment? Please don't say you've been hooked into reading Fifty Shades of Grey like my mother has!

Take care, honey. Hope the brats are being good!

Rach xxx

P.S: Did you hear back from the National Trust Property? Have you seen any other jobs you like the look of?

28th April

Dearest Rachel,
Thank you so much, darling, for a simply wonderful minibreak. I absolutely adored every minute of it and can't wait to join you in the future for further adventures. In fact I think we should make an annual event of it!

There were so many highlights, I don't know where to begin but I do feel special congratulations are in order over young Bertie. Why, he's a catch and a half! So charming, intelligent and he's obviously smitten by you. If you both need a place to stay while you're over for the Summer Fair let me know, as I do know your parents spare room isn't exactly built for two.
The theatre night was also divine and such a treat. I didn't even realize Barcelona had such a grand theatre. Next time I'm over lets go see the ballet there. Perhaps I'll have to do a winter weekend to see you and we could go to the Nutcracker, which I just adore.

Madrid was just wonderful also; so many beautiful sights and not only the buildings. I mean, are all Spanish men so dishy? You wouldn't get half the number of hotties walking round Brighton on a daily basis. In fact British men in general have never really done anything for me. In fact, Robert is one of the only ones that has ever won me over.

He collected me from the airport, the darling, and then once I told him about how you celebrate St. Georges Day, he went out and bought me twenty red roses. He has more money than sense, that man! He's very excited about Latchington Manor being opened to the public this summer but it's a big estate and I'm rather worried that he won't be able to handle it all on his own. I mean, it's fine if he just intends to open it once a month or for special occasions but if he intends for it to be a proper business and open for coach parties and such, he needs to get organized. The refurbishing has been excellent, though, and I dare say Latchington could make quite a profit if handled in the right way.

You, my darling, seem to be much more organized than he is. I was so impressed by everything Lucy and you had to tell me about your business and I was overjoyed not only to see the café but to be there with you when you first saw it. It's just perfect. The street, I noticed, wasn't far from one of the metro stops and there were other cafes near by but none will be like your little English Tearoom. Have you girls got any ideas what you're going to call it yet?

Hasta luego, darling,

Miss Elaine xxx

P.S: On the flight home I decided I'd direct Agatha Christie's 'A body in the Library' for my next production and that we'd do it the week of the Fair at Latchington Manor instead of the Village Hall. Thought it would make it a nice one-nighter and we could add our takings to the Cancer Care Fund. After last month's dire performance of 'Titanic: The Musical', they could do with a hit. I told Norman, the director, not to cast bloody Susana Isted in a lead role as she got stage fright but he wouldn't listen to me. He told me how well she auditioned and how she was sublime all the way through rehearsals but as I predicted, opening night came and she kept freezing and stuttering her words. She even vomited from the prow of the boat as it sank. The audience thought it was part of the

279

performance thank goodness!

30th April

Dear Rach,

Well, Master Yoda, speaker of wise words I have listened and realized that you are correct and you'll be pleased to hear I have snapped out of my self-pitying phase and moved into a new phase of positivity and enlightenment.

I began by eating the remaining chocolate ice cream from the freezer as it didn't make sense to leave the last few scoops there and then I made myself a few belated New Year's Resolutions, like you did. They are as follows:

1. Get the promotion and pay rise I know I deserve at work.
2. Stop dating boys and meet a man that's worthy of me.
3. Get a new hobby that interests me and introduces me to more people.

These three goals will be my new mantra and have been shared with my nearest and dearest, who have permission to spank me if I deviate from them or attempt to give them up.

Tomorrow I'm meeting with my boss to discuss number 1. Number 2 is on hold until I find a suitable candidate and number 3 is in the process of being decided. Suggestions warmly welcome.

Love,

Suz xx

P.S Thanks for being such a good friend. Love having you in my life, no matter how far way you are. Your support over the years has meant so much to me.

P.P.S: Your threat to pass on my address to Vicky Big Bum, however, was evil and cruel and I'd have never forgiven you if you had gone through with it!

Chapter 10
May – A Month Of Surprises

4th May

Dear Rory,

May the fourth be with you! Ha! I couldn't resist it. Mind you when you receive this it won't be the fourth any more so the joke might be lost. Anyway I know you're a Star Wars fan so thought you'd appreciate it! How are you, my darling? How did the big move go?

You know what I realised recently and that is that, out of our group of friends you're actually the first one to move in with a boyfriend, so that means you are now officially the grown up one. I wonder if you'll be the first to marry and have kids too! My goodness: Rory Harrison all grown up and settled down. I request the role of Head Bridesmaid. Sus will make a suitable bridesmaid, for sure, but you'll want someone who lives in an amazing city in Spain as Head Bridesmaid so the stag/hen do is guaranteed to be amazing! By the way do gays have a special name for their stag-dos?

You do realize that now you're no longer in the village you'll have to make even more of an effort to stay in touch with Suz and me, especially Suz as she's feeling the pressure of being a single girl in her 30's. That also means not just taking her out to gay bars as she'll never meet a suitable man there!

How's Harry? Will he be coming to the Summer Fair? I can't wait to meet him. I think Alberto is a little nervous about coming over. Meeting a few friends at a time is manageable but being introduced to a whole village of people could be a bit intimidating. I think he feels he's going to be unveiled or something or made to stand on stage as I show him off like a prize bull. The thought is tempting, though, as he's certainly a stallion and I am proud to call him my man - but at the same time I want him to feel relaxed. Perhaps I'll organize a few 'catch-ups' with people before the big day of the Fair and then he'll know a few faces and be a bit more at ease.

Lots of love,

Rach xxx

P.S: How's Mr. Paws? Licking or sniffing anything at the moment?

4th May

Dear Rachel,

We came home to find your letter and we're both so happy you've found a place for your business and with Miss Elaine's approval it's sure to be in a good location. As Phil and Kirsty always say "Location, location, location!" There's a lovely new little tearoom in the village but it's so out the way that it's too much of an effort to get to. It's right up near the old convent and most of the old biddies haven't got the puff to get there. I'm not really sure it will stay open long, I'm predicting it will be another estate agent in a year's time.

I'm glad you and Miss Elaine had a lovely mini-break. Madrid sounds wonderful. Perhaps one day your father and I will go there. I also like the sound of the high speed train, I'm sure it's a lot more stable then a Cruise Ship on the English Channel! We did have a good time but lets just put it this way darling I'm not sure your father and I have the sea legs to go on another one!

Here's a breakdown of our holiday with a few highlights along the way:
Day 1 Southampton: Departed and settled into our luxury room. Wasn't exactly like a suite on the Titanic but bed was comfy and we did have a little balcony. However if you dared venture out on the balcony you normally ended up almost being blown off into the sea, it was so windy. I'm sure if we had been touring the Caribbean you would have been fine but the British Isles are a little on the windy side!

Day 2 Guernsey: Had a delightful day on Guernsey. Beautiful island with a lovely main town with cobbled streets. Had a lovely seafood lunch near to one of the sandy beaches and your father and I went for a paddle.

Day 3 Cork: After a bit of a rough night we decided to skip the day trip to Cork and the Blarney Stone (why anyone wants to kiss a dirty old stone that thousands of other people have kissed is beyond me anyway!) and we stayed on the boat. Not sure if it was the choppy seas or the seafood from the day before but we both needed a quiet day.

Day 4 Dublin: Thankfully, we both felt much better the following day and went ashore to Dublin where we had a tour of the city, including the famous Ha'penny Bridge. That night on board they had a River Dance group perform in the theatre and that was indeed a highlight. How they can fit a theatre on a boat is beyond me but it really was impressive. When we headed back to our cabin your father insisted on River Dancing the whole way back!

Day 5 Day at Sea: Again the slightly dodgy feeling came back and we both felt like we were River Dancing the whole day. I distracted myself by attending a cookery demonstration and your father took himself off to the slot machines. The only trouble was, because we separated, we spent the rest of the day trying to find each other and then finally, when we did, we forgot where the cabin was! Don't get old, darling, it's a terrible business!

Day 6 Orkney Islands: These were your father's favorite. We spent the whole day on a bus tour of the island and even went on a boat trip to see some of the local wildlife. We then had an excellent afternoon tea and your father bought himself a kilt. I didn't really approve especially as he insists on wearing it true Scotsman style to the Village Fair in July! Heavens forbid it's a windy day!

Day 7 Inverness: This was another fun day as we headed to Loch Ness and your father took his best camera, trying to get a shot of the monster. At one point he thought he had spotted it, then realized it was a rock sticking out of the water!

Day 8 Edinburgh: This was possibly my favourite spot on the tour. The city was a joy to see and the shops were wonderful. There were plenty of street entertainers and we visited the castle to see the views. In the afternoon we went on a ghost tour and almost had a heart attack after someone jumped out at us on the final part of the tour. We were having so much fun, in fact, that we almost missed the coach back to the ship and we were the last ones on board. Someone tutted as we got on board the bus but your father showed them our winning tickets and told them as Luxury Cruise Winners we were entitled to keep others waiting. Your father has a great sense of humor when he wants to show it!

Day 9 Day at Sea: On the final night we had the Captain's Dinner and as we were Competition Winners we got to dine at the Captain's Table! I'm so glad I dragged your father round

Marks and Spencer's the week before and got him a new suit, as we were right up there with the Captain and some of the other special guests, including the Chef who did the demonstration. I wore a beautiful sapphire gown with pearl accessories and your father said he'd never seen me look so beautiful. It made my week. Even though he can be a right old pain in the neck at times he's a wonderful man and I do love him. Can't imagine doing things like that without him. Naturally he went and spoilt things by dropping raspberry coulis all down himself at dessert but nobody's perfect!

Day 10 Southampton: We finally arrived back at Southampton and, after ten days at sea, I have to say were pleased to be heading home. Again the Competition Company didn't fail to look after us and provided a taxi all the way home.

Naturally, I unpacked and started the washing as soon as we were in the house but I let your father have an afternoon snooze as a reward for winning the tickets for us.

It's certainly opened my eyes to competitions, darling, and I suggest you have a go, too. Who knows what you could win and in these times of cutbacks no one can afford to turn their nose up at a freebie!

Love, peace and happiness,

Mum and Dad xxx

P.S: I'm auditioning for Miss Elaine's one-night production of 'The body in the Library' tomorrow. She left a copy of the script in the letterbox for me while we were on holiday. Going to have a read through and give it a go!

10th May

Dear Rach,

I need to thank you so much, Rach, for putting in a good word for me with Miss Elaine regarding the new job Lord Robert has advertised. She rang me up last week and said that you had told her that I was looking for a new job. She then explained how Lord Robert (I have been told to just call him Robert but I still find it strange, so keep the Lord part there) needed someone to take over as manager of Latchington Manor; organizing events, planning educational visits and generally running the place on a daily basis. At first I thought it was a pretty crazy idea and did explain that I had little experience in such a role but then I thought about all the transferable skills I have and I convinced myself that, actually, it was the perfect job for me. I'm very well organized, used to planning, full of creative ideas, used to working with other people and have organized plenty of events before (World Book Day, Arts Week, Drama Workshops, Sports Day).

So the next thing I know is I'm being interviewed at Latchington Manor and after a cup of tea and a cucumber sandwich, the job is mine! The money isn't as much as I was on but Lord Robert said that, hopefully, if we bring in more tourists next year my salary will increase accordingly. To tell the truth though, honey, I'm just over the moon. It's the most amazing opportunity and after 11 years teaching it's just the escape I needed. I'm a little nervous as I'm not too sure where to start with it all but Lord Robert says that, over the summer we can sit down together and start making plans and then I'll officially start in September.

It will be brilliant, Rach, I'm so excited and can't wait to get going. I've said I'll help organize the Summer Fair, something I've done at Fairway Primary for the past 5 years, so I'm starting with you and Alberto, honey. I wondered if you'd do us the honor of providing some of your delicious cakes for a cake stall? I intend the Fair to have a traditional Great British theme with bunting and flags - but I'd also love a Spanish corner, so was wondering if your Alberto would cook up one of his paella's for everyone to enjoy. I could source the equipment for him if he could provide the cooking talent! Let me know what you think.

Thanks again my lovely. You don't know how much you've done for me!

Gemma xx

12th May

Dear Mum and Dad,

So glad you enjoyed your 'Free Luxury Cruise', I'm still green with envy but from the sounds of it, I might have also been green with seasickness too! The only time I've ever really been on a boat for any length of time was when we went to the Floating Bamboo Restaurant on Brighton Marina for my birthday once and I ended up having to leave as I felt like I was going to be sick. The humiliation of being probably the only person ever to get seasick whilst on a floating restaurant still moored to a jetty in a bloody marina! Talking of birthdays... It's my birthday in a week's time and I'm starting to feel a little nervous about it, to tell the truth. It will be my first birthday away from home and without my family and friends around me. On the plus side, though it will be my first with a boyfriend (I'm not counting Peter as he was a jerk) and I have a feeling he's planning something! I'm not sure what he's up to but Alberto has been acting a bit sneaky lately and was asking if I'd be working the weekend of my birthday or not. Thankfully I am not working and only have a couple of week's left of shift work before I can say 'Adios' to Madam Sanchez.

The last few weeks have been great but are starting to drag a little, if I'm honest, as I'm straining at the leash to get to work on the café - although, as I don't yet have the keys to the place, there's little point in getting my knickers in a twist at this stage. Lucy has been a star, though, and has had her head buried in all the paperwork for permits and licences and so on. Her Spanish has improved so much but thankfully we also have Maria to help us to double-check everything.

My Spanish is still frustratingly basic, it's a bit like a jigsaw puzzle; I have bits and pieces but not enough to solve the whole puzzle. I am enjoying my language exchange, though, and Maria is becoming a super friend. She's very patient with me and I'm sure I'm getting more out of the exchange than her but she says she enjoys it and I believe her. We start every session very seriously talking about what we've done that week in each other's language but then after about half an hour we crack up and confess to all the mistakes we've made and bloopers we've said. I'm much worse than her as I'm surrounded by Spanish people to make mistakes with but she's now using English much more in her job so has made a few of her own. For example, the other day while we were studying in my flat, she excused herself to go to the 'bog'. Apparently she's keen to understand slang and pick up 'day-to-day' vocabulary but she thought it was just another word meaning bathroom – until I corrected her and told her how 'rough' it sounded. She then blushed the deepest shade of red and told me that she had used it the day before whilst in an important meeting in front of about twenty English clients! How we laughed! Can you imagine telling a whole group of prospective clients you were off to the bog? LOL

Lots of love,

Rachel xxx

P.S How did the audition go? Did you get a part?

14th May

Dear Rach,

Happy Birthday my best buddy! Can't believe I'm not there with you to celebrate. I am, however, thinking of you and know that you'll just have the best time whatever you do. I hope you like the present - it's from Rory and myself! We didn't want to send anything too big so thought something flat was best, which was a bugger to find, actually. I'm thinking the world needs a shop that only sells flat objects that can be sent easily in the post to friends living abroad.

Just to update you on my personal goals... I got the promotion I asked for! It really does show that if you don't ask you don't get - yet if you do... I was very nervous and almost backed out but thought I needed to at least try, so spoke to my manager and explained my thinking and how over the last few years I had really made an impact on the company and was well respected in what I did. He listened and then said he'd think about it. Two days later he came to me and said that he agreed with me and was making me Advertising Manager for their new clients in the United States! He said the company had been thinking about exploring the US market for some time and this was a good a time as ever. He then said I had an upfront manner (He was possibly looking at my tits as he said that bit) and that the yanks would like that, so I would be their main advertiser for this important new phase in the company's history. I couldn't believe it, Rach; I'll get to go the States too! Perhaps I'll ask if my advertising support assistant Miss. Rachel Williams from the Spanish Office can come with me sometime!

Personal Targets 2 and 3 are yet to take off but what a great start. I'm off out tonight to celebrate down the pub with your Mum and Dad, actually. I decided, as your Mum was the one that started the 'Resolutions', she might as well help celebrate my achievements. Promise I won't get them too pissed!

Love you, darl!

Suz xxx

P.S Rory sends his birthday greetings and said he'd give you a buzz on the day. I accused him of being too lazy to send you a card but he says a personal phone call was more his style. Lazy bum, if you ask me!

15th May

Happy Birthday Darling!
21 again are you? That's what I always tell everyone. When you get to my age you actually stop counting and start going backwards. I'm possibly a teenager again from my calculations! What are your birthday plans, darling? I suspect they revolve around your gorgeous Spanish man. I'm sure he's got something exciting organized for you. I always say the first time a boyfriend gives you a gift, it's the telltale sign how much they love you. Don't get me wrong, though, it's not always about how much it costs, though that does count when you're receiving perfume - no one likes cheap perfume - but rather the thought that has gone into it. I was once given a goldfish in a bowl by a trapeze artist from the Russian State Circus. I wasn't really quite sure what he meant by that gesture so decided not to pursue the romance. If I had, perhaps I'd be touring the world as a Circus Performer now!

Have a drink on me darling!

Miss Elaine x

15th May

My dearest darling,
Happy Birthday! Hope you have a truly special day. Your father sends his love and asks if it's getting warm there yet. I swear he spends more time checking on what the weather is doing in Barcelona than he does checking the local forecast. He tells me it's going to be a sunny warm day for you so I said I bet you have a picnic somewhere. Do you remember that time we had a picnic for your birthday in Brighton and a terrible sea mist came in? Nobody could see a thing but we had prepared all the food so braved it and even though we could hardly see each other, still had a good time. I remember lighting the candles on your cake thinking that ships would think it was a lighthouse! By the way, your father is 70 later this year so we better start planning ahead. I know he's not fond of big gatherings but we need to do something special, so get your thinking cap on!

Last night we went for a few drinks with Suzy down the local pub. Well, I say a few, in fact it was a few more than a few. That girl is a bad influence on us but we both had a wonderful time, so much so, that today we've both had rather sore heads and stayed in bed until 11am! That's the longest we've ever stayed in bed but there was just no way we could get up. My head has only just cleared now and it's 5pm and your father is still wandering around like a bear with a sore head! It was worth it, though, as Suz has been promoted and she seems back to her normal self. I take no credit for her success but have to say my Resolution influence does seem to be making a difference this year. Yours have been so successful darling and now Suzy seems to be doing well on hers too. You need to ask her about her progress on her second and third resolutions too! I'm not one to talk but lets just say we bumped into Andy, the cameraman and after joining us for a drink, he seemed to be getting on pretty well with Suzy. She's even said she might pop along to Camera Club some time as she's always been interested in photography! Don't tell her I told you but watch this space!

Love, peace and birthday hugs,

Mum and Dad xxx

P.S: I spotted Victoria Plum and her drippy husband today but thankfully they didn't see me. Mind you, I did have to perform a series of manoeuvres James Bond himself would have been proud of. They were coming into Waitrose as I was about to leave so I ducked behind a stand advertising 'Back to School' equipment. 'Back to School 'in May? The poor teachers and kids haven't even broken up yet! How can they be going 'Back to School 'when they still haven't left? It's beyond me, all this. I bet you we'll have Advent calendars out soon! Anyway, after watching them head into the fruit and veg section, I then went to the furthest till to pay and after what seemed like an age, headed for the exit just as they appeared again. I then bent down pretending I'd dropped some money and after they headed up the cereal aisle, I made a dash for it! Told you it was like James Bond!

P.P.S: I've been told the first batch of our Pinup cards will arrive any day now for final proofing! Very exciting! I hope they've come out alright, I'd hate it if my wobbly bits were on show for the whole world to see!

P.P.P.S: I almost forgot to tell you that I got cast in 'A Body in the Library'! I'm going to be playing Dolly Bantry, a friend of Miss Marple and the wife of one of the suspects. She's a fun character to play and a bit of a busybody. Your father said it won't take much acting talent to play her! Cheeky man! Very exciting, I just hope I remember all my lines!

17th May

Dear Gemma,

Congratulations on the job, Gemma! As soon as I heard Miss Elaine mention that Lord Robert was after someone to manage the Manor I thought of you. I just know you'll make a success of it. With all your creative ideas you'll bring people flocking to see the place.

Have you told your evil Head Teacher you're leaving yet? I told Madam Sanchez about a month ago and she's virtually ignored me all month. I get the odd negative comment about my work or about how exactly I'm going to manage running my own business but apart from that I've continued doing the night shifts so have escaped most of her vile looks and poisonous comments. I really don't understand why people like that act the way they do. I guess they must be very lonely people.

We'd be delighted to take part in the Village Fair. I'll organize a bake off with Mum and Mrs. Ashley (still can't get used to calling her by her first name!) and together we'll bake up a table of goodies to sell. As for Alberto he's thrilled. He wanted to help out in

302

some way and cooking his paella for people to taste is right up his street. Perhaps I'll suggest he leaves out the octopus tentacles so it caters for British tastes more!

Lots of love,

Rachel x

22nd May

Dear Miss Elaine,

You were right about a boyfriend's first gift and Alberto didn't disappoint, not in the slightest. I had just finished three days of night shifts and was pretty exhausted so told Alberto I'd be happy with dinner out and then a quiet night in. He said he had booked the best place in town and told me to dress up. So I washed out my tiredness in a refreshing shower and put on the dress I wore to the Opera with you and we headed into the city.

We walked around for a while, enjoying the evening air, and then started heading back in the direction of the flat. I asked him where he was taking me but he wouldn't say. Then the next thing I knew I was standing in front of our café! Only it wasn't the way I had last seen it; it had been repainted and plastered, the original tiled floor had been polished, the counter was varnished and new shelves had been put up. There wasn't any furniture yet, apart from one single table and chairs with candles everywhere. Alberto, along with Lucy and Maria, had actually picked up the keys to the shop three weeks previously and whilst I had been working at the hotel, they had fully refurbished it. Needless to say, I burst into tears - in fact, I've not cried so much from happiness ever before. It was simply beautiful and Alberto had done it for me. I kissed him and then he sat me down and told me to wait for a moment while he organized the dinner.

While I sat and took in all the beauty of the room around me, I sipped at the glass of cava that had been presented to me and smiled. Now I could picture it all and I just couldn't wait to start shopping for the furniture and all the decorative bits and bobs. Alberto then appeared from the now functioning kitchen and presented me with plate after plate of delicious-looking home-cooked tapas dishes. There was the best jamon I've ever tasted, mussels in tomato sauce, calamares, chipirones (tiny squid), patatas bravas and slices of manchego cheese. It was just perfect.

I then unwrapped Suz and Rory's present, which he had secretly brought along, and discovered it was a set of gorgeous screen printed posters that would look perfect in the café. Following that I opened the card with the money that Mum, Dad and yourself had most generously put together for me so I could start buying the furniture we needed for the café.

Then last of all, Alberto gave me a final present from Mrs. Ashley. I carefully undid the tissue-paper wrapping to discover her recipe book. Inside were hundreds of carefully handwritten recipes for cakes, desserts, jams and all sorts of sweet things. I was speechless and even though I was miles away from all of you, I had never felt so close.

At the end of the evening, Alberto explained how Lucy, Maria and he had organized getting the keys, how they had kept me under the illusion of having to wait and how they had worked together getting everything ready. Alberto then explained that before he started work each day, he had secretly taken my mail from the postman when he knew it to be a present, so he could have it waiting here for me to open. I told him that I was about to write to Suz explaining that the present had obviously gone missing, as it wasn't attached to the card she had mentioned it in, but then I understood why that was! Should I be worried or happy that my man can obviously fool me so easily?!

So there we have it. A wonderful birthday I will never forget. Tomorrow Lucy and I are going shopping to buy our first pieces of furniture for the café! I'll send you a few photos once we put it into place.

Lots of love,

Rachel xxx

26th May

Dear Mum and Dad,

Thanks so much for the money for the café. Lucy and I have had a three day spending spree and thank goodness she has a car because we've filled it to the brim each time. We decided to go to a variety of different places, as the look we are going for is Traditional British Tearoom with a modern twist. If you picture the café in Friends (relaxed and comfortable), mixed with the Dining Room of Downton Abbey (traditional and British), and add in a slice of Great British Bake Off (colourful and fun), that's pretty much the café we aim to create. I know it might sound eclectic but Lucy and I have exactly the same vision and after the past three days we have pretty much everything we need. There's lots of work still to be done, however, as it's a mixture of new things from IKEA (It's a bloody awkward place to go round but it does have some affordable goodies) and old flea market stuff that either needs restoring to its original state or upcycling into something new and beautiful.

We ended up getting the following things:
- 6 small wooden tables from IKEA.

- 12 chairs of various state and design from different flea markets. (We still need a further 6 and Alberto's going to also make us a wall bench too)
- Cutlery - a quality silver traditional set that just needs a good polish.
- Crockery - various floral and decorative plates, saucers and bowls from various shops.
- 20 picture frames of differing size, colour and shape from IKEA for a picture wall I intend to hang.
- A beautiful glass cabinet for our cake display along with 10 cake stands from a lovely local kitchen supplier that I'm sure we'll be revisiting time and time again.
- 6 gorgeous kitsch floral trays from Habitat.
- 20 meters of Cath Kidston-style fabric (though much cheaper) to make up table cloths and napkins.
- Bathroom bits and bobs for the loo.
- An amazing old fashioned Victorian style till (which was pretty pricey but will look great on the counter).
- Then all the bits and bobs for the kitchen for my baking. Those were some of the priciest things but are an absolute must for all the

baking we're going to be doing.

So there we have it. Our tearoom is shaping up nicely; next week we're going to find our suppliers and then all we need is a name for the shop. You're usually great with things like that Mum so get your thinking cap on and let me know.

Lots of love,

Rach xxx

P.S: Will you help me bake up a storm when I'm back for the Village Fair? Gemma has asked me to supply a table of treats and I think I might need an extra pair of hands. Was thinking of asking Mrs. Ashley too. Do you think she'll be up to it?

P.P.S: Loved hearing of your James Bond skills for avoiding Victoria Plum and Kevin. Next time I suggest you simply take a stun gun with you, tranquilize them and shove them in the freezer with the Raspberry Pavlovas!

28th May

Dear Rach,

Lovely chatting the other day, honey; so glad you had a wonderful birthday. I can't believe that man of yours! Could he be anymore perfect? Sounds like you had a super time and from the sounds of things your café will be open in next to no time. Have you come up with a name for it yet?

I also realize that I do, in fact, owe you an apology or two for getting your parents pissed last week and for not mentioning Andy in my last letter. As I said on the phone, though, I did have my reasons and I stand by them.

Number 1: Your Dad might be the quiet one but you know what they say about them. He bought as many rounds as I did and, in fact, it was your Mum that suggested we open a bottle of bubbly to celebrate. How was I supposed to know she'd get as bubbly as the champagne we had? Hee, hee!

Number 2: I didn't mention anything about Andy because I normally shout my mouth off about a guy and by the next letter its all over and done with. No this time I want to take my time, see how it goes and not act like a crazy loon! He isn't anything like the guys I usually go for, though, Rach. He's a bit of a nerd, his body is quite average (not that I've seen all of it yet!) and he's quite normal looking and yet there's something about him that makes me really like him. He also makes me laugh.

Not that I'm shouting out about it but I'm seeing him again this week and I'm also going along to the Camera Club! God, what's become of me?! Your Dad is chuffed, though. He said the Club needed some totty! Cheeky bugger! I'm looking forward to it, though. Might be something new to get into and at last I can use the £300 camera my parents bought me for Christmas two years ago that's still in its box.

I guess unexpected things happen for a reason and we should embrace them when they do.

Love you,

Suz x

28th May

Dear Rory, Harry and Mr. Paws,

I just wanted to write to you congratulating you on moving in together. I hope he's behaving, Harry; I think he's house trained (and I'm not talking about Mr. Paws!) You must be over the moon to be living together. I hear the move went relatively smoothly and that you seem to be settling into your seaside life pretty well. I love Brighton very much, it's such a fun and creative city. I suspect in a few years you'll be having one of those open house days for the festival and proudly be showing off your original art prints as well as your fantastic taste in furniture and accessories, which is why most people really go to those events; to snoop round your house! Talking of original art, I love the prints you and Suz got me for the café. They are just super as whenever I look at them they remind me of home. Luckily for me, Lucy isn't really into all the decoration part of the business; she always takes an interest but, thankfully, lets me make the final decisions.

In fact, the shop is only about a couple of months away from opening, which is so exciting - and now that I've finally finished at the hotel I'm free to

313

devote all my time to it. I practically skipped out the door when I left. I'll miss the doorman Carlos but as for Madam Sanchez, she hardly even looked up from the front desk. She merely asked me to let Carlos return to his work and if I could move from the exit as I was blocking the way. Such a rude woman! One day, karma will come and bite her in the butt, I'm telling you! Still, I don't need to worry about her any more as I'll be my own boss from now on!

Lots of love to you and the boys,

Rach xx

29th May

Dear Rachel,

I fear I may have missed your birthday but simply had to write to you wishing you a special day. I'm sorry I've not written before but after the way you ran off from me at Christmas, I felt a little bit silly about writing to someone who obviously didn't feel the same way as I felt about them in return.

I've often thought about our kiss at Christmas and just wished I had done it sooner. You looked so gorgeous that night that I knew I had to give it a go. I just wish you had told me you had met someone in Barcelona. I hope I didn't ruin anything for you. The way you ran off to meet him I presumed he must have meant a lot to you. I was secretly hoping that perhaps I had been wrong but from the sounds of things you're pretty loved up!

Anyway, I hope you are well and that you are happy with your new man in Barcelona. I heard you were coming back home in a month to come to the Summer Fair. Perhaps we could meet up, as friends of course, I'd like to see you.

All my love,

Marcus x

P.S: You looked bloody amazing in the Cinderella dress!

Chapter 11

June – Marcus 'bloody' Flynn

1st June

Dear Gill (Mrs. Ashley),

Thank you so much for your recipe book. It was the most unexpected and delightful gift. I promise I will cook every single thing in it and perfect each and every recipe. I was also pleased to see there were some free pages too so I can add my own recipes to it. The other day I baked a toffee cake with a caramel apple filling. It was divine! When I'm over in July, I'll bake one and bring a slice round for you and Tom. Talking of July, would you be free for a couple of days before the Village Fair, to help Mum and me prepare the cakes for the cake stall? Trying to cook enough cakes by myself might be pushing it for time, so I thought between the three of us we might be able to do it. Let me know what you think.

Mum told me a few weeks back that the first batch of Pinup cards were on their way. Have you seen any yet? I'm rather nervous about having anyone see me virtually naked, yet I'm also incredibly excited, as I just know they'll look amazing and make a fortune for the charity. Will you talk on the day of the Fair or will you get Tom to make a speech instead?

Love from,

Rachel xxx

8th June

Dear Suz,

You won't believe who wrote to me last week. Marcus bloody Flynn! I'm still pondering how to reply - or even if I should - but after such a heartfelt letter I feel I suppose I should at least make the effort to respond. He starts innocently enough, saying he wanted to write to wish me a belated happy birthday, but then goes on to explain in great detail how much he cares for me and wishes he had made his move earlier. Naturally, he mentions the kiss and how it made him feel when I ran off after Alberto. Obviously he never saw me fall or Alberto leave otherwise he would have stayed around. He knows I'm coming back in July and wants to meet up 'as friends' yet signs off: 'All my love, Marcus'.

Oh Suz, why did he have to write? I'm deeply in love with Alberto and in no way am I going to ruin things with him again - yet I have - and always have had - these feelings for Marcus that don't seem to go away. I feel terrible for the way he's feeling now but also think he had plenty of opportunities to say these things to me while I was in the UK or to have written to me before. Why now? Why would he do this just as I'm so happy?

I am happy, though, so will just have to tell him that, I guess. Yes, things could have been different but that time has gone. I'll tell him that I'll see him but I'll also make it clear that I now have someone else in my life. I've not mentioned anything to Alberto; I hope that's the right thing to do.

Lots of love,

Rachel xxx

P.S: He also commented on how good I looked in my 'Cinderella dress', which really means he was talking about my breasts!

9th June

Dear Marcus,

Thank you for you birthday greetings and for your letter. The words meant a lot to me and I read it several times. I'm sorry I didn't really get to see you again after Christmas but things were all a little confusing for me and I just needed some time alone.

I sorry if I hurt your feelings, though, and perhaps if the timing had been different and I hadn't moved to Spain, things would have worked out differently. However, I now have a boyfriend and we are very happy together. You're a lovely man, Marcus, and I'm sure you have a whole line of ladies wanting to date you. Perhaps when I'm back for the Village Fair in July we can meet up and I'll help pick out the best one for you.

Take care and thanks again for the letter,

Rachel x

10th June

Dear Rachel,

I'm only going to write you a short letter as in a week or so we'll be in Barcelona with you! We're both very excited! I feel a bit naughty having two holidays so close together but as the last one was a freebie it doesn't really count.

Your father and I were very impressed with how much you've organized and done in such a short amount of time on your café. Miss Elaine says much of the hard work is also down to Alberto; he sounds like a very useful fellow indeed. Very wise getting together with someone who is good with their hands!

I love the sound of the café theme and have been thinking of suitable names, so let me know what you think about the following: (I apologize for some of the latter entries but your father insisted I add them to the list just in case you wanted something more 'unusual'!)
- *A Slice of Heaven*
- *Little Britain*
- *A Piece of Cake*
- *Let Them Eat Cake*
- *The Tea Cozy*
- *Rachel's Place*
- *Sponge*
- *Tea and Cake*
- *Cake Hole*
- *The Jaffa Cake Café*
- *Shove It Inn (That's when I told him to stop as he was just getting stupid!)*

By the way, I'd be glad to help you with the Village Fair cake stall and I'm sure Gill would love to as well. She's not been too well lately but, hopefully, now she's had her three chemo sessions, she'll start to improve. She says she's got more tests early next month so we'll have to wait and see.

The play is going well, sweetheart. We have rehearsals twice a week and your dear old mum is doing pretty well. I seem to be managing well with the lines but keep forgetting where to come in and exit. Miss Elaine told me the other day I walked off through the spot where we'll have a wardrobe! I guess once we transfer to Latchington Manor for rehearsals next week it will become easier.

Love, peace and happiness,

Mum and Dad xxx

P.S: The Pinup cards have arrived and they look amazing! Not a wobbly bit in sight! We've been given some sample packs before the main batch arrives for the Fair so we can start advertising. Tomorrow morning Miss Elaine, Suzy, Gill, Fat Janet and myself will meet with the local papers for an interview. Hopefully that way, they'll print a good write up and we'll be able to get more people to come to the Fair and in turn raise more money and awareness for the cause. I'll also pop a pack of the cards in my suitcase, darling, so you can see them for yourself very soon.

12th June

Dear Rachel,

I'm so glad you liked my gift to you. That recipe book was first given to me by my mother when I was twelve years old. I had just discovered the delights of baking and she told me that if I wanted to learn how to bake properly I had to note down my own recipes and adjust the ones in the books to make them better than the ones already written down. And that's what I did. Some of the cakes and desserts are more successful than others but you'll see a little star rating system next to the best and worst ones. See if you can improve on my recipes, Rachel. It would make me feel very happy to know my recipes were moving on to others to be cooked and enjoyed.

As for helping, I'd love to, Rachel. I'm currently feeling a little weak after a funny few days but by next month I'll be right as rain and ready to get baking. If you need to use my kitchen, just let me know and I'll give it a tidy before the week of the fair.

Thank you for writing, Rachel. It's so nice having something in the post which isn't a bill or an advert persuading me to buy something.

Love and best wishes,

Gill xxx

15th June

Dear Rach,

I can't believe he wrote to you. Number 1: I'm surprised he can write and number : what did he think would come of it? While you were single and free to date he was all over that skinny leggy supermodel of his and as soon as you went away and found love of your own he's all interested! I don't really get it. I think it's a classic case of a man wanting something he can't have. When you were single he was free to flirt with you whilst also dating Lucinda but then as soon as you became unattainable he wanted you for himself. Now don't get me wrong, he is an absolute stud and I would have encouraged it if you were still here, honey, but since moving to Barcelona, you've grown and changed and now have Alberto and you no longer have any need for the Marcus Flynns of this world. I think you did the right thing writing to him, though, and there's no harm in meeting up - but remember, honey, for years he held onto your heart and even now he has a piece of it - I guess all crushes do - so when you see him again I think you should take it back. Let go of the past and move on.

Listen to me! I came over all relationship Guru! I guess I've had enough failed ones to know what to do and what not to do though, honey. Thankfully I seem to have made a change myself and things are going really well with Andy. We've been out quite a few times now and done things that I've never really done before. We even went to a comic convention! It turns out he's a bigger geek than I thought and loves Super Heroes. I was dreading it but it was actually a really fun day. It was in central London and he showed me all the main characters he likes and we saw a clip of one of the latest movies; we then had a great lunch out in Covent Garden and as I had been patient all day, taking an interest in comic book things, he took me to see Wicked! It was indeed wicked and, again, I'm just surprised that someone so normal is actually really rather special. That night we went back to his and I pretended to be Wonder Woman for him! He liked that very much and I have to say I think I brought out his Incredible Hulk! I have a feeling I could get into the Super Hero thing after all.

Love,

Suz x

21ˢᵗ June

Dear Rachel,

I've just bought a copy of the local paper and was shocked to see pictures of you and your mother posing without your clothes on. Why on earth would you both do something so stupid? What goes in print stays in print and those near pornographic images will stay with you both for the rest of your lives. Didn't you both think what people would say? I, for one, would never do something so frivolous and even if I did, Kevin would have forbidden me from exposing myself for everyone to see.

I understand that the 'Pinup Cards' launch at the Village Fair is yet to happen, which is a blessing in disguise; and that is why I'm writing to you, to implore you and your friends to think twice about selling those cards. Why you can't go round with a moneybox like everyone else, I don't know! Make the right choice or I'm afraid you'll face public humiliation!

Kind regards,

Victoria

26th June

Dear Victoria,

My name is Derek Williams and I am the husband of Penny and the father of Rachel, I am also the friend of Gill Ashley, who, sadly, died of cancer yesterday. Gill was a wonderfully kind and gentle woman who brought joy and friendship to so many people's lives. In life she will be remembered for her kindness to others, her positivity even in the face of having this terrible illness and for truly being someone who saw the beauty in life.

I read your letter with great sadness and disappointment that someone could be so narrow-minded and uncaring. Your letter contained words like "stupidity", "humiliation" and what other people may think. Well, I'm writing to you to tell you that I couldn't be prouder of my wife, daughter and their friends. Truly brave women who are willing to bare not only their bodies but also their vulnerabilities to the world to make a difference to people's lives and to beat cancer. Not once in your letter did you mention the word cancer or charity. These two words are why those cards were printed and why those cards will sell by the thousands at the Village Fair. I personally will be manning the stall and trying to persuade

329

as many people as possible to buy cards with pictures of wife, daughter and their friends, not only to make money to support cancer charities but also in honour of the memory of the wonderful woman who we all called our friend.

Kind regards,

Derek Williams

28th June

Dear Miss Elaine,

What a week it's been! The beginning of it was so happy as Mum and Dad had just arrived and there were so many things to show them and tell them. They met Alberto and, naturally, loved him and then we took them to see the café, which is now all kitted out with everything we bought. Then we had the phone call from Tom to say that Gill had died. She had apparently got an infection and as her immune system was still low her body just couldn't fight it. It all happened so quickly.

I am just thankful that Mum and Dad were here with me at the time. Dad was just brilliant; he looked after us both and also gave Tom all the right advice and support that he would need. When they left I felt so sad — I would have said empty but Alberto was with me, and having him there was just everything I needed.

I managed to change my flight so that I arrive a few days earlier than planned so I can attend the funeral. Alberto is coming with me, too. I spoke to Tom to say we were coming and he told me to bring a cake. He said that he had been given strict instructions by Gill to not make her funeral a wake but instead a celebration. She had apparently made plans just in case and had stipulated that we all wear colours and bring a coloured balloon to release into the air. It doesn't surprise me really as she was such a lovely women, always smiling, so why shouldn't her send-off be the same.

Perhaps, Miss Elaine, if you're free you could collect us from the airport? We'll both have large suitcases and as we're staying with you it might just be easier than asking Mum or Dad.

I hear the Village Fair will be celebrated in Gill's honour. I'm sure she would have loved that. I'm determined to raise as much money as we can for Cancer Care. We might not have not been able to save Gill but perhaps we'll be able to save the lives of other people suffering from cancer.

Lots of love,

Rachel xxx

Chapter 12
July – Best In Show

9th July

Dear Gill,

Well I think would have enjoyed your send-off, Mrs. Ashley. As requested, we all turned up in bright colours, carrying our balloons. Your husband wore a bright yellow suit - which I believe was your favourite colour - he looked very smart, even if he did insist he looked like a canary. Miss Elaine wore bright pink, as did Suzy, who never wears pink. Mum wore a gorgeous purple dress with a lovely feathered hat and Dad wore shades of green. I looked like Miss Scarlet from Cluedo in bright red. The rest of your family and friends looked amazing too and hundreds of your ex-pupils turned up as well. Between them all, they were decked out in every colour of the rainbow.

You'll be pleased to know the sun came out and after the service, where your sister read a prayer and Miss Elaine read a poem, we all released our balloons into the air. It looked simply beautiful. As instructed, all the members of the camera club took amazing photos as the balloons took off and everyone cheered. I won't lie to you: there were plenty of tears too, instructions or no instructions, Mrs. Ashley: people still cried.

The celebrations were not over yet, though, as the celebration of your life continued with a tea party. Your baking skills were renowned not only in school, Mrs. Ashley, but also amongst your friends and family and so we all brought along a cake from the recipe book you gave me. The week before your funeral, I copied the entire book and sent one recipe to each of the guests and asked them to try their best to bake it. The results, if I'm honest, were varied but that made it all the more fun. I naturally baked your classic Chocolate Cake, which came out triumphantly, unlike Suzy's version of your Upside Down Cake, which looked as though it had been dropped off the table a few times.

At the end of the celebration your husband stood next to your beautiful Pinup Photo and gave a lovely speech and we all raised a toast to you. I won't repeat the words he said, as I'm sure you heard them for yourself but his final ones resonated with us all. " Live each day of your life as if it were your first and your last." Something we all need to do, I think.

Tomorrow is the start of the Village Festival and there is a lot to do. A national newspaper picked up on the Pinup Project and since then the village has been buzzing with excitement and requests for further articles and even, possibly, a TV crew. Looks like our aim has been achieved after all.

Love, peace and happiness,

Rachel xxx

16th July

Dear Rachel,

What an achievement dear! In total, the proceeds from the Village Fair, combined with the totals from the opening of Latchington Manor, the production of 'The Body in the Library' and the sale of the Pinup Cards raised over £20,000! This week we're going to have one of those huge cheques made up so we can present it to the Head of Cancer Care. Gill would have been so proud of us. It makes me smile thinking about all that we've achieved over the last week but there's that deep sadness there too. I guess though that it will pass and that she was right to have insisted we celebrate her life. What's the point of it all if we can't feel happy about what we've done in life?

Your cakes went down a treat, my love; it was blooming hard work trying to get them all done in time but we certainly did it. Just as well we asked around for an extra pair of hands; Fat Janet was indeed the perfect pair we needed and boy could she bake! A pity she's not thinking of moving to Barcelona - she would be a surefire addition to The Tea Cozy Café. I love the name by the way, much better choice than the ones your father was suggesting!

By the way, what did you think of my performance in 'The Body in the Library'? I was so buzzing at the end of it that I really didn't take in what anyone said; and then the rest of the week was all cakes and cards and reporters so I didn't even think about the play. Miss Elaine was ever so pleased with us all and Lord

Robert suggested it become an annual event, that your friend Gemma could organize with the local society once she took over the Manor Manager role. Exciting times ahead, I'm sure!

Love, peace and happiness,

Mum and Dad xxx

P.S: You must thank Alberto on behalf of everyone. That boy is a saint, the way he got stuck in with helping and sorting out all the tables for the fair - and his paella was incredible! Some of the Flower Club biddies turned their nose up at it at first but then were soon tucking in once they smelt it cooking. You really did make the right choice there, my love. I knew he was the one for you as soon as I realised he could put up with your father speaking loudly and slowly at him for a week just in case he didn't understand English. If he can put up with your father he's a keeper in my eyes!

18th July

Dear Suz,

Well, honey, I'm back in Barcelona and do you know what? It feels like home. The last few weeks have been so emotional and I thought perhaps that coming back here I might feel lonely but I don't. It feels like I'm where I ought to be, especially after finding out what a lying sneaky bastard Marcus Flynn turned out to be.

If it hadn't been for your lovely Andy, we would have never had known. I can't believe he was boasting about sleeping with me before the end of the week; how he should have done it before I left but he decided that Long Legged Lucinda was easier, so he'd stuck with her instead and would have me at Christmas! I also can't believe he saw me fall over and walked off; after all, who would want to sleep with a girl with a fat lip and broken nose? He then timed his letter with my arrival back in the UK so I'd be emotionally ready for him! Little did he realise that, even without knowing all this, I would have refused him because I was in love with Alberto, a man he could never even hope to be. Bad luck on his part for boasting in front of Andy and not realising the two of you were dating, and that he would immediately tell you (you've got him well trained). My reaction was ok, wasn't it? I know it did cause a bit of a scene but personally I thought a cake in the face followed by a knee to the groin was justified, don't you?

Naturally, Alberto asked me what it was all about and I told him everything. I was a little scared he'd think that I cared for Marcus but he did his usual thing and kissed me and then offered to punch Marcus in the face if I wanted. I did want, in fact, but decided it wasn't really needed, especially as the press had just arrived to interview us about the Pinup Cards. Despite my concerns, the Pinup Cards looked magnificent. My bottom actually looked pretty firm; must be all the flights of steps I climb in my flat, and thank goodness my muffin top was well hidden! I'm over the moon with how many packs we sold and how much money we raised. The spokesperson for the charity said our donation would make a big difference to cancer awareness in the local area, something I know Mrs. Ashley would have been proud about.

So my lovely, are you all ready for your summer

holiday? Only a week to go until you and Gemma come over! Make sure you bring plenty of sun-cream, please, it's hot at the moment and I don't want to be hanging round with a couple of lobsters for the next couple of weeks!

Lots of love,

Rachel xxx

21st July

Dearest Rachel,

Well what a couple of weeks we've all had; the play, the fair, interviews about the Pinup Project, and the funeral. Rest in peace Gill.

I still can't quite take it all in, everything happened in such a whirlwind of events. After the funeral, my mind switched to putting on the play, which I have to say went better than expected, considering the lead-up to it. Felicity made a marvellous Miss. Marple, don't you think? I've always admired her timing and diction. She could have made it big, you know but decided she didn't want to become an actress and was happy to bring up a family instead. An equally demanding role! Your mother was also wonderful, not a natural actress, between you and me, but she certainly made up for lack of acting talent with volume and enthusiasm. Robert was over the moon that we used Latchington Manor, though, and after talking to Gemma she seemed rather keen on making it an annual event, which would be terrific.

After the fantastic turn out for the Village Fair, Robert is going to keep the Manor garden's open for August, then once Gemma is working full time will re-open the house with a Gala evening in September. Apparently she's already found a jazz band to perform at it. I think that young lady's going to bring plenty of life to the Manor.

I'm still in total shock about the National Press coming to cover the launch of our Postage Pinup Cards; I wonder who contacted them? Perhaps the local press passed the story on. Whoever it was, though, deserves our thanks as the donations to Cancer Care have been through the roof. In the last 5 days alone the total has shot up to £50,000! Your mother is beaming. Certainly showed those old biddies in the village a thing or two. They've even asked a few of us if we'll go on This Morning and be interviewed by Philip Schofield! Naturally we're all rushing to have our hair done ASAP, can't go on National Television looking a mess, can we? Tom is coming with us too to talk about Gill; after all, she was the one who inspired us all in the first place. It's a pity you won't be here, darling, but I know you've got exciting plans ahead of you also.

I saw the photos of 'Tea Cozy Café' and it looks amazing. I've decided to come over in autumn to sample some tea and a slice of your Victoria Sponge Cake. You'll also have some flowers arriving the day before the opening on the 1st, darling. I was going to keep it a surprise but I thought if they arrived the day before, you could put them out on the counter and the tables to give it that extra 'je ne sais quoi!'

Time to go, my dear; the weather is fine and Robert wants to fit in a round of golf before lunch in Bosham. Haven't been there in years and absolutely adore the place, so thought we'd go walk round the harbour, feed the swans and enjoy fish and chips in the local pub.

Write to you soon,

Miss Elaine xx

24th July

Dear Rach,

You'll be pleased to know that I've not done any more baking since Mrs. Ashley's farewell. Never mind Apple Turnover, more like Mrs. Ashley turning over in her grave if she could have seen what I did to her cake! I'm sure she would have laughed, though; she was always such a kind lady and one that saw the best in all people.

Not that I'll ever be as kind as her but it's certainly good to have something to aspire towards. I have to say, after you stuck that Victoria Sponge in Marcus Flynn's face then kneed him in the balls I was as happy as could be! Not that I'm a violent person but boy did he deserve that. He'll also have a hard job getting another date round these parts no matter how much he uses his good looks as I've told everyone on Facebook what a total sleaze he is. You see, Rach, Social Networking does have his uses! Hee, hee!

I'm proud of you though, honey, you had made up your mind even before seeing him again that he wasn't the guy for you and you chose right. Alberto is just the nicest guy and also a good influence on Andy. When he saw Alberto carrying around three tables at a time, whilst he struggled with just two, Andy said he might join the gym and tone up a bit. I suggested that if he felt Captain Catalonia was looking good after his gym sessions, perhaps the Hulk could as well! Never underestimate the powers of Wonder Woman!

Well darl, I'll see you a few days after you get this card, I expect. So I suggest you stock up on sangria and fill the freezer with ice-cubes!

Hasta pronto chica!

Suz xxx

25th July

Dear Rachel, Penny and Derek,

Please accept my deepest sympathy for the loss of your friend. Please also accept my apology for being the most selfish, judgemental bitch possible. Your father's letter to me made me sit up and think about what a prudish cow I had become. I looked back at my life and thought about the decisions I had made and the person I had become and realised that my perception of what I should be like was based on what I thought others would think of me rather than what I felt was right or even what I wanted to do myself.

I had a long talk with Kevin, who told me that I had indeed become - in his words - a 'miserable old bag' and that he had become afraid of telling me because of the way I might react. My own husband had become afraid of me! So I decided to break down the barriers I had put up, to right the wrongs I had done and bloody well let some fun back into my life.

With Kevin's consent, we sold our 'Old Farts' camper van and gave the money to Cancer Care. I then contacted the National Press and told them that they must go to Latchington Village Fair where the most remarkable women were gathering for the launch of their Postage Pinup Project. and that they'd be fools not to feature it in their papers. We then contacted your friend Suz, who put us into contact with Andy, the cameraman, who then came and took our photos··· in the nude, Pinup style! Kevin insisted on joining in as he said maybe it would promote greater awareness of male cancers and I totally agreed. That's probably why your jaw is still on the floor after seeing our picture on the front of this card. We decided it was only fair to send the first one in the pack to you before we sent the rest to our friends and family asking them to donate some money to the charity. As you can see, I decided to pose with the laundry basket whilst Kevin held the peg bag!

I'm not expecting your forgiveness so soon after my recent behaviour but, hopefully, one day you'll write to me as a friend.

Love from,

Victoria Plum A.K.A Vicky Big Bum xxx

31st July

Dear Rachel,

Happy Anniversary, darling! One whole year in Barcelona and what an achievement that is. You do realize that even though we miss you terribly we are so very proud of you. When you first told me you were thinking of moving to Spain, I selfishly wished it wouldn't happen as you'd be so far away from us but as the year has gone on and we've seen all the things you've achieved, I couldn't be happier for you.

I know how much you love Great Britain and I can see how much you enjoy coming home to us but I also remember how stressful life was here for you and how unfulfilled you felt in your job and with life in general. But now we look at you and see you with a wonderful boyfriend, learning a new language and in charge of your own business and we know 100% you made the right move.

Now before I cry all over the letter and smudge the ink, I must tell you some shocking news. As you know Miss Elaine, some of the other Pinups and myself, are heading up to London this week to be interviewed by Philip Sconefield! Well the first thing we all did was book into Sally's to have our hair done. Whilst there, however, the new girl, Jessica I think her name is, was so caught up in all our news that she put the wrong hair dye on Betty Potter's hair. Poor old dear had the foils removed to discover that instead of being her usual harvest brown she was pineapple blonde! Well, after the initial shock and a cup of tea and a chocolate hobnob, she decided she looked pretty good for a 95-year-old and said she'd have the same again next time!

Will write to let you know how it goes on This Morning. Your father is more excited than me, says he'll get to meet that Holly Willoughby. Little does he realize that she's on her holidays at the moment!

Love, peace and happiness,

Mum and Dad xxx

P.S: Good luck with the big opening next week! We'll be thinking of you and your friend Lucy. Your father and I will have a cup of tea and slice of Bakewell Tart in your honour!

P.P.S: Wasn't it funny that your Carrot Cake won 'Best In Show' in this years Village Fair. Gill would have been proud of you! Some things are just meant to be!

Postscript

August – A Piece Of Cake

st August

Dear Mum and Dad,

I can't believe I've been in Barcelona one whole year! Today is my Spanish anniversary! Hooray! So much has happened since moving here I just can't quite take it all in.

- I've made new friends like Lucy and Maria.
- I've started to learn Spanish and have now passed two exams and even though I'm still a bit on the crappy side when it comes to speaking, I understand a lot and I'm much better than I was when I first arrived.
- I survived working for the Boss from Hell and even after all her criticisms and put-downs, I remained respectful and professional. (I'll leave karma to take that bitch down!)
- I've settled into a new home and have developed a great friendship with my neighbour Belen.
- I joined a gym. Fell off the rowing machine, tripped on the treadmill, got swept into a whirlpool of Spanish grannies — and still I go each week in the vain hope of one day having a flat stomach!
- I've successfully started my own business and today we had our first day of trading — and it was great!
- I have an amazing hunky Spanish boyfriend who

loves me more than patatas bravas and whom I
love in return.
- I've successfully maintained and strengthened
  my relationships with my family and friends
  from back home.

All those things in a year Mum! I remember this time
last year saying goodbye and feeling so nervous. I was
anxious about whether I was doing the right thing
and now, a year on, I know I have. I still miss you
and Dad and all my friends so much but I know that
you're near at hand and only a phone call or a letter
away. I know that I can survive without Facebook,
Twitter and Email and that my life has been all the
better for it.

Today when we opened 'The Tea Cozy' and all our
friends gathered round as Lucy and I cut the ribbon
to the shop, I knew we'd make it a place for talking
and laughing, a place where people can come and write
letters to their loved ones and even post them, seeing
as we have a postbox right opposite the café. We're
going to encourage people to put their phones away
and to read instead and our embryonic café library will
increase, especially with Alberto on hand to put up
new shelves whenever we need him. Most importantly,

though, it will be a place to eat cake: cakes from Mrs Ashley's recipe books and from my own head; and they will be so good that nobody will ever feel the tiniest pang of guilt about having a second or even a third slice.

Today we hired an artist to paint a message onto the café window. It reads ' Live each day of your life as if it were your first and your last. ' The perfect motto I feel for what we should all do.

Love, peace and happiness,

Rachel xxx

ABOUT THE AUTHOR

R. W. (Richard William) Mitchell was born in West Sussex in the UK, where he grew up in the little village of Storrington and took part in the local Amateur Dramatics Society.

Later in life he trained as a Primary School teacher and lived in Brighton on the sunny South Coast of England.

In 2011 he moved to Barcelona in Spain, where he now lives with his partner and writes in between trips to the beach and visiting the local cafes.

In his spare time, when he's not writing, R. W. Mitchell loves going to the cinema and baking cakes that look like cowpats, and he greatly enjoys reading.

This is his first novel for adults but he has written a number of children's books. Unlike Rachel, R. W. Mitchell is on Facebook and Twitter so feel free to look him up and send him a letter.

Made in the USA
Charleston, SC
07 December 2015